Spell

By

Tamsin Johnson

Part One

Quaintlip Village, 1757

"Ugh, the stench of it!"
The young woman, sickly-looking already, twisted on the stool towards the damp wall and covered her mouth, suppressing the retching which threatened to turn her stomach inside-out again for the fourth time that morning. It was a well-practiced exercise. Once the heaving sensation was under control, she glanced warily back to the steaming wooden cup of leafy mess proffered to her from across the kitchen table.

"What you put in it, anyways?" Wren had one grimy hand clamped over her mouth, her voice stifled.

"Family recipe." The older woman with the long black hair answered plainly, leaning forward and holding the cup out before her still, unfazed by Wren's nausea. " Drink it down quick, in one go, like. Soon be over then."

And she nodded her conviction at Wren , her deep-set, dark eyes fixed on the girls' own. Wren had never seen eyes such as these before here in Quaintlip; she had been born and raised and married here, and she knew the villagers like her own family. Folk here were tawny-skinned from lives spent working on the land, surely, but not like this woman. She was swarthy and other-worldly, with hooded eyes circled in deep shadow. Her thin shoulders were hunched like those of the buzzards that Wren had seen away on the wild heathlands outside of the village, beyond the arable lands surrounding it. Wren half-expected to see talons at the ends of those long fingers, but

1

the woman's nails were short, and blunt, with a pale crescent like the moon on each one. Wren was conscious somehow that she did not want those fingertips to touch her own when she reached for that cup held out to her, in the same way that she would avoid touching a spider or a snake. The thought made her shudder inwardly.

Wren gazed around the room doubtfully, stalling for time suddenly, her courage waning as she observed the collection of dried leaves and berries, feathers and bleached- white bones strung from the mighty beams supporting the low, sooty ceiling. A muddle of brown bottles and stone jars cluttered the mantle above the open fireplace. A starling's head lolled from the neck of one such bottle, the rest of its body presumably pickling within the cloudy vessel. A ragged posy of tooth-edged leaves stuck out of the top of another: these were the makings of the recipe that the Volk woman had stewed in a blackened pan over the flames.

"Grown right here in the garden!" she had announced with pride, stirring the vile-smelling sludge.

"If you can call that a garden." Wren had thought, recalling the wilderness she had silently observed beyond these claustrophobic walls as she and the Volk woman had made their way discreetly around the back of the crumbling old house a short while earlier. *"No flowers and not one eatable thing in sight, far as I could see."* Just some woody, sour- looking herbs, and weeds, and a dank, gloomy well which gave off a fetid stench, causing Little Wren another retching episode as she hurried past, her shawl wrapped tight across her swelling stomach.

Wren looked away from the curious and disquieting contents of the Volk family kitchen. She had known, after all, not to expect roses and dainty chinaware in this place. Not with that name, not with those stories. People travelled from afar to visit Volkspell House, or, as it was referred to more simply in the village in lowered tones, the Spell House. She steeled herself mentally. She could not bear another child. Seventeen, and two babies not yet walking at home already. The second birth had almost killed her with blood-loss and fever. Her cheek still bore the imprint of the blow her hateful husband had dealt her that very morning on his way out to work in the piggeries. He had woken with a crippling sore head from an evening spent soaked in ale at The Feathers ,and their youngest was screaming heartily in the corner of the one room they all occupied. He hated going to the piggeries, and he hated Wren and, sometimes, she believed, he hated their two tiny girls too. "They'll be no bloody use to me when they're grown!" He would frequently slur at his wife after such an evening's activities. "Get 'em married off quick and out o' my 'ouse, like your father did o' you. The only bloody use for girls."

"'Urry up then," the crow-faced woman interrupted Wren's thoughts. "Drink it down quick, like. You'se paid your coin for it now, after all." And she winked slyly at Wren. "Might even be able to find you somethin' for that bruise. Or for your 'usband, if you unnerstand me?" She grinned then, a sudden and shocking smile which lit up the room like a ray of sunlight bursting through storm clouds. Wren's heart lifted at the sight of it. She found herself surprisingly at ease in an instant; conspiratorial almost with this strange woman who obviously perceived Wren's dire circumstances. She sat up straighter in the wooden chair, returning the Volk woman's smile. She took a deep breath in, raised the wooden cup, closed her eyes and gulped the contents in one go, forcing as much down as she could before the sickness and retching took hold of her again.

"There you go, then." The Volk woman smiled down at Wren approvingly. "Won't be long now."

The young woman gasped, the instantaneous cramps in her stomach powerful and terrifying.

3

"Can I stay here until…until it's over ?" she trembled, gripping the table edge with both hands.

"'Course!" The Volk woman grinned again, seemingly unperturbed by Wren's rapidly increasing agony. "Of course you can." And she sat down opposite the girl at the table, her eyes intent upon her sweating face which was drained of colour, her eyes stricken with terror.

"After all, we'se friends now, aren't we?"

Part Two

"Your destination is on the left."
Cerys Thomas reached a hand to silence the sat nav on her phone, wedged in to place beside her on the passenger seat with sweatshirt, canvas bag and water bottle. She turned off the ignition at last and exhaled relief: she had started out her journey with a fatigue that seemed to be ingrained in her very core, and it had been a long drive. Many long weeks had led up to this mini exodus out of London and away from her home. Mum had wanted Uncle Dom to come and collect Cerys: Cerys had refused. She needed her freedom as she expected her uncle did too, and she did not wish to be a burden while she stayed at his home all Summer. She had driven carefully, avoiding the motorway, and had stopped for coffee when she felt her concentration dipping. Hence her journey had taken a little longer than planned but she did not mind– she was on no schedule and the evenings were staying light and warm as Spring unfurled its delights.

Cerys glanced briefly out of the passenger side window and cringed inside. Her uncle's house was only a few doors down from the turning circle opposite the village pub, The Feathers. The circle, which was common land, also served as a small street-facing beer garden, and there were several locals sat at the wooden trestle tables, enjoying the last of the day's sun. Cerys was conscious of several pairs of curious eyes upon her, over the rims of pint glasses.

She gathered her phone and keys, and resolved to return to the car later for her luggage, envisaging her trainers and hairbrush and books all tumbling out of the top of her broken-zipped holdall as she lugged her belongings up the road in front of the audience. She made her way to Uncle Dom's narrow house with its lovely old red bricks and sash windows squeezed in mid-terrace as though it eternally held a deep breath. She lifted the silver door knocker, feeling suddenly shy, but the door was flung open before she had time to knock.

"Cerys! I was getting worried!"

"Sorry," laughed Cerys, stepping inside. "Were you waiting behind that door by any chance?!"

"Shush, you." Uncle Dom hugged Cerys with gladness: he was tall, and supple as a willow, and his height combined with Cerys's petite stature meant that he ended up embracing her head in a loving squeeze. Cerys grinned, her shyness dissolved, face pressed into the chunky grey wool of his jumper.

"I got a bit waylaid," Cerys stepped back, swiping her hand over her face, feeling the imprint of the cable-knit on her cheek. "North Circular. Usual gridlock. Had to stop off at services aswell."

"Have you eaten?" Dom asked. "I'll put the kettle on. Ring your mum and let her know you've arrived in one piece."

Uncle Dom's kitchen was small – the entrance room to the house, which was one of a row of old farm labourers' cottages. It was crowded in a pleasing way with a tiny pine table, two mis-matched chairs, and a battered bicycle leaning against various sheepskin and rain-coats hanging in the nook under the wooden staircase, climbing steeply to the first floor. Le Creuset pots and pans stood gleaming in vivid blue and mustard yellow array on shelves above a Butler sink. Dom filled an orange and black kettle ("Halloween Tea!" Cerys thought, grinning to herself) and set it on the hob, saying " Have a seat, if you can find space." He placed an enamel biscuit tin on the cluttered

6

table before her. Cerys sidled in to an unsteady chair and sent a message to her mother in London.

"Just got here, Uncle Dom is OK, all good, call you tomorrow x x"

The kettle began to squeal softly and Uncle Dom ventured: "Dare I ask…Should I be making you coffee this late in the day? I'm guessing it might not be helpful?"

Cerys grimaced and shrugged her shoulders, spreading her palms upwards in a gesture of helplessness. "It won't make any difference either way, Unc. " Cerys replied. "I think I've tried everything. Lavender oil, yoga, relaxation music, the sleeping tablets…I go to sleep just fine – the problem is the waking up in the small hours and then…" She tailed off, frowning down at her hands where she picked at a splitting nail.

Dom, sensing his niece did not want to elaborate further, shook his head in sympathy and set down two steaming mugs on the worn table top. "Well hopefully the change of scene might make a difference. Break the cycle, you know? And you have eight whole weeks ahead of you before college starts. I'm jealous!"

"Thank you, Uncle Dom," Cerys said seriously. " I do really appreciate being able to stay here. I know you're not exactly blessed with space. I will try and be a bit invisible."

"Nonsense!" her uncle replied. "Be as visible as you like. It'll be good to have your company. And if it goes any way towards alleviating your mum's worries about you then it will be a joyous thing for all."

*

"Going to put some cards up in the village for the gardening while you're here, Cerys ? Set yourself up for Horti college a bit?"

Cerys and her uncle were eating breakfast at the kitchen table next morning: Dom had made scrambled eggs on bagels with butter and grated cheese. She had slept surprisingly well for once, perhaps due to the combination of her long drive the previous day. Dom was going away for work at noon and would not return until the following evening. He worked sporadic and lengthy hours for television studios during filming with live audiences, which meant he could often be away for days at a time. He insisted on giving his niece a guided tour of the village before he left. The community store had irregular opening hours, he'd said – "We'll go and check the A-board outside." He also felt he should introduce Cerys to his elderly neighbour, Mrs Devin, whose equally elderly dog Flowers was to be found frequently wandering the streets of Quaintlip and would possibly need to be returned home in Dom's absence.

Cerys had visited her uncle several times since he had bought the house in Quaintlip village, of course, but always with her mother, and only for the day or overnight once or twice when Cerys was tiny and could still fit on the little sofa downstairs to sleep.

She had never come to stay before like this, on her own, as an adult. It had been loosely suggested by her mother that Cerys would help her uncle to get his garden in order while she was a guest there; gardening being one of her strengths and pleasures too. Cerys was looking forward to doing so for Dom. She agreed with him wholeheartedly that it would be sensible to try and earn some cash for when she started college, although that seemed an age away just then. There were bound to be people in the village, most likely the elderly, who cherished their gardens but were unable to do on-their-knees weeding and digging. Plenty of folk could not afford or did not want to hire from a company who would send a small team out to do the work quickly and efficiently, but who would not take the time to chat about

8

the roses or how best to keep slugs off the hostas, or whether there would be a hose-pipe ban that summer, and who would charge them a small fortune too.

After breakfast, Cerys hunted around in her bags in the spare bedroom , and found some of her contact cards, printed with her name, mobile number and service, and sunflower logo. They had helped her on the way to saving towards the car and driving lessons over the past year or so. A school friend's mother had been her first customer and she had distributed a few of Cerys's cards amongst her friends, and Cerys had built up quite a busy round of Saturday afternoons in various outdoor spaces – a tiny courtyard garden, one vegetable allotment, and a long, narrow strip of garden backing on to the railway line going in to central London. She was keen to work and eager to learn, and there was no room for boredom when each of the gardens were unique in their way.

She pulled on high-tops and large sunglasses – the sun could be agony on her eyes after a few consecutive nights cheated of sleep, and it was looking like it would be a bright day indeed.

"Ready?" Uncle Dom held the door open for her, locked up, and they headed out into a mild, still morning which held all the promise of Spring.

Cerys did not recall having noticed on her previous visits how pretty and well-loved the majority of the gardens were in Quaintlip (a name which had always faintly amused she and her mother, although neither could really fathom why.) Each one was as individual as the house they belonged to, and even the old workmen's terraces, which had no front gardens at all and whose front doors opened directly on to the narrow pavement, displayed colourful troughs beneath their windows that were abundantly filled with lent lilies and hyacinths, and primroses with pastel shades of lemon

9

and peach petals snugly crowded amongst crinkled, velvety leaves of apple-green.

The village itself had first become noted as far back as the thirteenth century, and many of the older properties still bore their original titles relating to their long-dead occupants' roles in Quaintlip's working life. Names such as The Tanner, The Tailor, The Smithy and The Parson's Lodge were engraved above doors and on brickwork. The main street was landmarked in the middle by the pub, The Feathers, and the grassed turning circle/beer garden, where Cerys had left her car the evening before.

Cerys and her uncle walked first to the end of the high street where more modern houses stood, with the small community shop which also served as a café and post office. Cerys pinned one of her cards to the notice board outside, smiling to herself as she read some of the other notices: "Grazing for One Pony available June, Harpers Farm, " "Chimney Sweep," "Fish and Chip van Fridays only, outside the Feathers@7pm" and "Book Club, Wednesday evenings at the parish hall." Cerys did not know why but it heartened her to know that such things existed, although she knew she would probably never have reason to make use of any such services.

They chatted lightly as they strolled, hands in pockets, back up the road on the opposite side this time, and Cerys wondered as she often had over the years why her uncle should be alone, delightful and easy company that he was. Perhaps, she hoped, he was simply content with his life and his interests, and kept himself to himself through choice. She knew that he had a strong, quietly-heeded Christian faith as did her mother, and Cerys understood well enough that this in itself was sustenance enough for believers, despite not being fully convinced in the matter of faith herself.

10

Uncle Dom pointed out the various footpaths as they walked, which lead to the ancient church upon the hill behind Quaintlip, and to the next village, Marsh, some seven miles away across the fields. Then they turned right at the furthest end of the high street where there was a small pond bearing early marsh marigolds on a smooth, murky green surface, and a picnic bench besides the pond where they sat down opposite each other to bask in the Spring morning for a few moments more.

Dom secretly observed how drawn and serious his niece's face was, despite her light-hearted conversation and seemingly relaxed demeanor. Cerys was naturally slight of frame but looked even further reduced in size recently: shadows had appeared underneath her once-sparkling blue eyes and hollows beneath her previously-rounded cheekbones. Her heavy, square-cut fringe accentuated her now-angular features and her straight, copper-coloured hair had lost some of its warmth and shine. He silently prayed that her stay with him would help to heal her spirit somehow, plagued as she seemed to be by whatever was causing her insomnia and the slightly haunted, distant look in her eyes when she was unguarded.

Dom and Cerys's mum, Nancy, suspected the episode to have been triggered by the death of their own mother early the previous year. All her life, it had just been Cerys and her mum together, with Nanny Grieg in the flat below, and Dom, a satellite, in orbit further afield. Cerys had spent much of her childhood in her grandmother's flat whilst Nancy was working long shifts at the hospital: grandmother and granddaughter had an inseparable bond. The small family grieved – were still grieving, of course – but Cerys had just gone…quiet. She withdrew into a private place of sorrow which she would not share. Then, last September, Nancy had messaged her brother to say that she was taking Cerys to the GP, that she had not slept a full night in weeks and was struggling to function throughout the day as result. They had arranged to postpone her start at college until the following school year. Cerys had been both relieved and a little lost, as friends began their new paths in life and she remained static, and somewhat isolated at home.

Dom's mobile rang suddenly, shrilly, in his pocket, and they stood up to resume their walk, the peaceful spell broken. Cerys spotted a tired-looking notice board across the road and went over to pin another card upon its pin-holed and weathered cork face. She was stood before the last of the terraced cottages on that side of the road, before the high street led out of Quaintlip, and became the main route to the next village. There was just farmland from here on, apart from one solitary house, set back from the road and almost obscured by a great gloomy screen of leylandii hedge, ten feet high at least.

With her uncle fully engaged in his work call, Cerys strolled casually up to the perimeter fence in an effort to take in the view of the front garden, which was chest-deep in herbs and wildflowers and weeds growing magnificently out of control. Bees sailed lazily from purple campion flowers to early poppy heads with their fragile, pale orange petals, and around white nettles and brambles all tangled and competing for space and sunlight. The antiseptic, sweet scent of rosemary and lavender rose up from the scene of outrageous abandon with the warmth of the day. Small birds busied themselves noisily in the tall grass, gathering material for their nests. Bindweed curled around every stem, suffocating yet beautiful in its way, with blowsy white trumpet-blooms and curvaceous vines.

Cerys gazed on, fascinated by the sheer scale and variety of plants in the rambunctious garden. The house itself looked empty, run-down and almost sagging with the weight of time. Dark beams dipped across the square face of the building where ground had shifted and the floors sunk over the centuries. Large sash windows stared blankly out over the wilderness, two-up and two-down, and all four oblongs of filthy lead-framed glass were crammed within by rioting house-plants, sweating against the cool glass. The front door was tiny – the house built long ago for smaller and more slender generations – and it's sage green paint was peeling like a bad sunburn. That door seemed to Cerys as though it belonged to a doll's house, or the backdrop of a stage set.

"Thinking of taking that one on?!" Uncle Dom joked, suddenly at Cerys's side. She shook her head, eyes wide, gesturing at the enormity of the project.

" It's empty?" she asked.

"Yes, has been for decades," Dom replied. " Some issue with the estate when the last owner died. It was a family home by all accounts, got passed down through the generations, and when the final member went it was unclear as to who the land should have gone. It's been so long now that nobody in the village knows anymore. But nobody will be pestering the authorities as the locals are terrified the land will be auctioned off to for development."

"I guess.." Cerys murmured. Sad, though, to see the place so neglected, the family hearth gone cold and the rooms within empty and lifeless. But all those house-plants? Behind those blank sash windows, something thrived there still? She held the thought vaguely in her mind as she and Uncle Dom walked back to his house. It clung there, wavering like a strand in a cobweb, shimmering and faint in her consciousness all that afternoon, as she waved goodbye to Dom from the kitchen window, after promises to ring her mother that evening, to eat something substantial for dinner, and to knock on Mrs Devin's door if there was an emergency.

Cerys settled on to her small bed in the box room that evening with a big mug of tea and a packet of biscuits, and idly began to watch a film she had seen before on her laptop. Her attention drifted to the pale blue Fleur de Lis pattern on the curtains and then to the black metal of the tiny fireplace, glinting in the muted late afternoon sunlight.

As she often did these days, Cerys felt sleepy far too early – the result of many wakeful nights which would leave her feeling ragged and wretched by mid-afternoon. In truth, she was dreading spending the night alone at her uncle's home but had resigned herself to the awareness that the problem was just as likely to occur at her home in North London, surrounded by a city full of folk, as it probably would do in Quaintlip, with its population sparse by comparison.

The problem manifested itself whether Cerys's mother was home, or whether she was working nights at the hospital and Cerys was alone. She did not mind solitude ; in fact she treasured it at times, and she was not afraid of the night as such but what came with it.

When Nanny Grieg had died, something Cerys could not explain had entered her world. An oppressive and ugly presence began to announce itself into her formerly restful nights with a sudden and sickening awareness. In the early days, it would cause Cerys to jump from her bed, scrabbling for light switches, her back to the wall in blind panic.

Some nights it crept insidiously into her dreams like smoke tendrils, bringing her to consciousness with her heart thudding and her throat dry, unable to move for fear of whatever the vile entity was in her bedroom. As the pattern progressed, Cerys became accustomed to it's arrival, waking less stricken with terror and more mentally resigned to the weary battle of wakefulness ahead which would last until daybreak. The atmosphere dissipated with the light, apparently chased away by the dawn and the gradual increase in traffic noise and the sounds of stirrings in the flat above as the children woke and television was switched on.

Cerys always knew that "it" would be there again the next night, and the next, but she could not allow herself to fall asleep in it's presence, no matter how exhausted she became. She did not understand a great deal about it but she felt in her soul that to do so would be dangerous; that she would lose the battle in some way to this phenomenon which had singled her out for some kind of psychological and spiritual attack.

She could not tell her GP the exact details of what was happening to her- she did not wish to be given a blanket diagnosis of depression, or bereavement difficulties, or teenage anxiety. It was not as simple as that, although Cerys could understand that health professionals would label her with all those symptoms. She could not envisage antidepressants being helpful in her situation.

"Exercise," the GP had recommended briskly, tapping at her computer keyboard . " A gentle walk before bed time to relax your mind." Kilburn however, was not so soothing, despite its many attributes. The off-licenses and grocery stores were open twenty-four-seven, people stayed out on the streets throughout the night and even after car-traffic had eased slightly the night-buses, police cars and food delivery mopeds still held their noisy influence over the roads.

Here in Quaintlip though, Cerys thought, they were worlds apart. She hoped that perhaps things might not be so draining. The nights were shortening, and she thought she might have a chance to regain enough sleep to build up her inner strength again, maybe even enough to shake off this whole miserable episode like a prolonged bad dream. The idea of walking out into the cool, silent solitude of the village after dark suddenly drew her like a charm. To be able to tread quietly, unseen, alone with her thoughts under the pure black, star-struck sky, breathing the clean air that Cerys imagined could only feel like velvet on her skin, would be a delight.

Cerys drifted into sleep, and awoke some hours later to find the room in darkness and her laptop out of battery. A thin icy crescent of moon was strung high up in the night sky. Revived and now wide awake, she surrendered to temptation and ventured out, finding the silence of Uncle Dom's house a little claustrophobic in his absence.

She closed the front door as softly as she could - the peace of the village was intense, almost tangible – with every noise magnified in the stillness. Cerys trod lightly up the high street, self-consciously imagining pairs of eyes behind net curtains observing her strange nocturnal activity. She grinned at her own paranoia in the darkness.

The Feathers was long-since closed up for the night and the empty tables silhouetted on the little green. Cerys was startled as church bells chimed deafeningly once- one a.m.! She had not realised it was so late – or early. Clapping a hand to her mouth, she fought the compulsion to laugh out loud, her nerves jangling at the sudden clang. " Night-walking alone and laughing out loud." Cerys berated herself silently. "Not a good first impression of the new-comer for the locals."

Cerys strode on, more purposefully now, inhaling with deep pleasure the scent of the fields, sweet and damp and fresh. She reached the edge of Quaintlip, where she and Dom had sat briefly the previous morning. She crossed over as they had done yesterday in order to walk back down the high street to his house when she remembered the abandoned cottage behind the leylandii hedge. Cerys was unable to resist a sudden desire to see the place under the moonlight, as if she might steal a glimpse of the past somehow, concealed ordinarily during daylight hours.

16

The impression of the cottage being guarded by the towering hedge was even greater to Cerys in it's nocturnal state. The leylandii appeared denser, the shadows blacker within, like a fortress shielding a fairytale castle, she thought. She crept around to the gate which opened on to a cracked flagstone path. The lines of the stone slabs were softened by couch grass sticking up and low, frothy mounds of fleabane, which were ice-cream pink and white in the day but jagged charcoal and silver now.

Cerys could picture vividly in her mind's eye the garden as it had been centuries before - a real kitchen garden, and the vital heart of a country home where villagers in an isolated hamlet such as Quaintlip provided for themselves and bartered produce with their neighbours in order to get by. Hens would have pecked amongst sorrel leaves and cabbages, gooseberries grown fat on spiny bushes next to sprawling raspberry canes and, later on in the season, damsons and crab apples would have weighed down the branches of the now-blossoming trees growing to the right of the dwelling. Potatoes would have sprouted from the banks of muddy trenches and feathery tops of carrots – indigo in colour back then, not orange – would stand like flags in rows between.

Perhaps the inhabitants of this property would have traded eggs and plum jam and penny-bunches of green mint at market a day's journey away by horse and cart, Cerys pictured. They would have risen with the dawn chorus and returned, weary-eyed travellers at dusk to dying embers in the hearth, a kettle of rosehip tea to warm themselves, and straw-stuffed mattresses on which to sleep.

Cerys, still lingering at the gate, closed her eyes, hypnotised for a moment by her inner vision. Breathing out a lungful of cool night air, she opened them slowly, her gaze upon the face of the darkened house. Her heart seized suddenly and viciously in her chest. There was a face in

17

shadow at the top right hand window. Moonlight picked out the faintest whites of a pair of eyes, a line of scalp, and, maybe, just maybe the dimmest glimmer of a tiny candle or lamp. Before Cerys could even blink the figure was gone and the window was black and featureless once more, save for the silhouettes of the ugly house-plants writhing and crowded behind the pane.

Cerys recoiled, her tranquil moment vanished, replaced instantly with acute self-consciousness, her skin prickling and her limbs stiff. She had thought herself completely alone on this moonlit walk, the village in slumber and she the only intrepid voyeur delighting in her solitary rambling. Now she felt to be a trespasser, caught-out and in panic -the house she had believed to be empty had been watching her all along. And the face at the window had looked...*furious.* Fear bubbled up fiercely inside her like acid and Cerys fled. She ran from the cottage and the wild garden all the way to the other end of the high street, back to her uncle's house, her footsteps now echoing in her ears like thunder as they pounded the silent black road.

*

Cerys did not sleep for the remainder of that night, or the next. Having bolted herself safely back inside Uncle Dom's house, she huddled under her duvet, leaving the lamp on the side table switched on for comfort. She tried desperately to evade the mental image of the face she had seen – or thought she had seen – seething with fury- *at Cerys!* - and distorted by moonlight and shadow. She felt the presence of the familiar fearful atmosphere descend upon the room like a damp and suffocating fog. It was though "it" sensed Cerys's shaken state of anxiety and latched on to it in parasitic fashion.

18

Cerys read, skimming over paragraphs in her fatigue, until dawn when she heard the first of the bird's chorus begin. Only then, with a thin line of milky daylight on the horizon, was she able to relax into the sleep she craved, with the knowledge she had gained over the past year and a half that the unseen attack on her would slink away with the light.

Cerys slept until lunchtime that day, stayed in her room reading and dozing until evening, then drove to the nearest Co-op some miles away to pick up milk and chocolate. She attempted to sleep the second night with little success.

How could she close her eyes when she was so very afraid of something she could not even see or name? Who could she go to for help with such a vague explanation of the problem? Not the police, not neighbours, not a hospital. Her mum did not doubt her, for which Cerys was deeply thankful, but it did not make it go away. The frightening vision at the window of the old abandoned house in Quaintlip just compounded Cerys's misery. She couldn't exactly ring her mother up and tell her she'd been night-walking in the village and had a scare. Her mum was already so worried about her, along with working her long shifts nursing people with far more tangible and physical afflictions, and this latest drama was more than Cerys felt able to burden her with.

Uncle Dom returned at noon, earlier than expected, dropped his bags to the kitchen floor and exclaimed upon seeing his niece " Good grief! I told your mother I'd left you in a reasonable condition – and now look at you! What happened?! Bad night?"

"Something like that," Cerys instinctively shied from the subject, simply glad for her uncle's presence. Although not an overly tactile sort of person he was not unaffectionate, and his practical and cheery nature were reassuring.

"Have you actually eaten *anything* other than Digestives while I've been away?" Dom asked, as Cerys helped him carry his bags through to the living room. She answered with a guilty look and grinned, and he glanced at his watch.

" I think The Feathers is just about open," Dom said. "Come on, let's go. I'm starving. Tired of catered food. I've not eaten a decent meal in two days!"

The Feathers had indeed just opened up for the afternoon and Cerys and her uncle ordered toad-in-the-hole with buttery mash and thick gravy, and it was glorious. They sat back after eating, replete, and sipped their pints, enjoying the sensation of full stomachs and pleasant company in the ancient, low-ceilinged pub. Cerys's past two sleepless nights eventually began to catch up with her and she found herself rubbing her dry eyes, yawning behind her hand.

Uncle Dom became drawn into a lengthy discussion with a neighbour about a proposal to install speed bumps on the high street. Cerys politely excused herself, and slipped away from their table and back to the house where she removed her boots without hesitation, climbed the creaking stairs and curled up on her soft blue duvet, having drawn the curtains against the mid-afternoon sun. Sleep hit her like a wave, and slammed her headlong into blank unconsciousness.

*

It was some hours later when Cerys was startled awake by a loud knocking at the front door. Her heart thudding, she struggled to gather her thoughts as she sat up. The sun had dimmed, and she had slept much longer than she had intended. Uncle Dom had apparently not yet returned from The Feathers, and anyway, he had his key, of course. It couldn't be him banging on the door like that. Cerys went downstairs, still foggy with sleep. The knocking was persistent and impatient, irking her before she'd even reached the bottom stair.

Cerys opened the door halfway, cautiously, to reveal a young woman, slim and dark- haired, with a slightly stooped posture which gave the impression that she was already leaning forward as if to walk straight past Cerys and into the house.

Cerys stiffened defensively, her hand still upon the door frame. "Personal space?!" she thought, incredulous of some people's rudeness.

"You the gardener?" the woman asked, or rather, stated.

"I am?" Cerys answered, wanting to add rudely, "What's it to you?"

"I'm up the road," the woman said, smiling a little, jabbing a thumb towards the street. "I'm sure you must've spotted my place. Needs some work. Saw your card up in the village."

"Oh...OK," Cerys said hesitantly, relaxing her grip on the door frame a little. "Well...when would you want me to take a look at it?"

"Today," the woman answered without hesitation. "Can you come today?"

("Absolutely no social skills!") Cerys thought fleetingly, trying to process the abrupt introduction. She fleetingly wondered whether it was a countryside manner that Cerys wasn't accustomed to yet? "Er...I can come up tomorrow and see what needs doing and if I'll be suitable?" she offered. There was no purpose to her making arrangements to start a job if it transpired that the woman wanted a tree felling or some other unmanageable task. "Plus...it's a little late to start working now?"

The woman had not yet taken her foot off the doorstep and was still angled forward as if expecting to be invited

21

inside. She frowned momentarily at Cerys's attempt to stay her, and in that moment, an image flared brightly in Cerys's mind of a feral dog, teeth bared and growling, poised the second before it lunges to bite. But the woman only grinned, suddenly and surprisingly, a beautiful smile that seemed to reach almost from ear to ear.

"Yes!" she said, "That'll do. It's the last house at the end of the high street. The one with the very high hedges. And I'm Theresa. Come in the morning." And she turned and strode away back up the road, shoulders hunched as if against a cold wind.

Cerys shut the door, and stood with the late afternoon sunlight pouring through the kitchen window onto the red tiled floor. She wondered briefly if she was dreaming, or asleep still, so bizarre was the encounter. The house with the tall hedges, the leylandii reaching darkly to the sky – the house Cerys had fled from. The woman – Theresa -must have meant that one... yet it could not be, because surely that house was empty, deserted for decades?

*

Uncle Dom returned around nine that evening, alerting his niece to his presence by the sound of his front door key missing and scraping the lock several times.

"Three sheets to the wind!" she exclaimed, as she opened the door for him, using her grandmother's famously nonsensical term for a person having been drinking in earnest.

They broke up with laughter in the open doorway, shushing each other simultaneously which only served to make them louder and more obvious to the rest of the quiet street. Cerys steered her uncle into the kitchen by his elbow and pulled out one of the rickety pine chairs where he sat down heavily, with a scraping of its legs on the tiles which made her grimace.

22

She felt the uncomfortable knot of anxiety that had been building inside her ease a little, as she made coffee for them both and they recounted other peculiar sayings belonging - as far as they both knew – solely to Nanny Grieg. It made Cerys feel nostalgic and happy and desperately sad all at the same time.

She spoke about her prospective new job to Uncle Dom, and the odd manner in which it been instigated. Dom had since navigated his way into the front room and now drifted in hazy comfort in his armchair. In a lazy voice, eyes closed, he said "Funny how we were just talking about that place. It must have been sold at last." And then, with mock solemnity he pointed a finger at Cerys, who was curled up on the floor cushions. "Heed your withers!" He said – another senseless yet perfectly valid saying of his mother's, meaning simply to trust one's instinct.

"Ha!" Cerys laughed. "I'd forgotten *that* one!" It was late now, and as she made her way upstairs to bed she resolved to do just that. She would go along to the last house at the end of the village, meet that Theresa woman again, establish the priorities of what needed to be done in her garden (it was possible, Cerys thought, that it might just be too much for her to manage by herself anyhow) and if she did not feel comfortable she would politely decline to return, saying it was too big a task for one person.

"I'd probably really need a skip to clear it, and hedge cutters, and God knows what else," Cerys told herself as she turned the lamp off and awaited sleep. "Beds and borders, that's what I do. I'll tell her that tomorrow." And she sank into slumber, and dreamed of an empty house with all its windows broken, and of a ragged grey bird at her bedroom window, head tilted, beak askance as it watched her sleeping from the other side of the cold glass.

*

23

"Luck!" called Uncle Dom, upon leaving for a trip into town the next morning. "Heed your withers!"

"Ha ha," Cerys grinned, checking over her collection of hand tools, gloves, and twine, crammed into the back of her car. A ridiculously short drive to the end of the village but necessary nonetheless with all her gardening paraphernalia in tow. She pulled up to the frail-looking gate of the old house, and took a deep breath, gazing up at the monstrous hedge which nearly obliterated the bright warm sunshine.

Cerys pushed the gate and went to the front door, stepping over grasses and mint and daisies spilling over the worn stone flags of the pathway. Vegetation rose waist-high on either side of her. She jumped, startled briefly as she reached the stone steps to the front door: a large frog, disturbed from somnolent contemplation amongst the broken plant pots, leapt right across her feet and vanished into the long grass.

"Must be a pond here somewhere amongst this lot," Cerys thought, as she knocked briskly on the spongy, peeling wooden door.

"Cerys Thomas, we met yesterday, good morning!" she announced brightly as the door inched open with a painful creak. To her surprise, the woman who stood before her hunched in the dark hallway, was very elderly, with thin grey hair scraped back tightly into a bun, and a black shawl wrapped around her concave shoulders. She wore a long, billowing kind of a house- dress, grey with polka dots, the kind that Nanny Grieg's mother and grandmother wore in the sepia-toned photographs from their family album.

"Oh!" Cerys faltered, her fleeting moment of confidence apparently gone. "I was expecting to see the other lady – Theresa? I'm here to look at the garden."

"Trayza's not 'ere," the woman said without a smile. "Trayza's out. You can wait in 'few want."

24

Nothing appealed less to Cerys just then; the gloomy hallway, the sullen old lady, a home in darkness on a bright Spring day. She offered her best cheery smile and said, "I'll have a look at the garden shall I? While I wait? See what I can do out here?"

" 'few like." The woman barely shrugged, already turning back to the cool shadows indoors. She shuffled slowly away without another look at Cerys, leaving the door slightly ajar.

Cerys watched her vanish into the gloom, breathing a quiet sigh of relief. She turned to the garden – where to start?! She had never seen so many weeds. And the tumult that was outside seemed continue without pause on the other side of the house's filthy windows with all the bloomless houseplants snaking upwards, seeking and stealing the light.

Cerys began by stamping down a vague path to an aged compost heap by the farthest wall from the house – somewhere to dump the green waste and burn the dry stuff. She tugged a rusty old wheelbarrow from a mound of nettles and disentangled ropes of bindweed from the wheel.

"A bit of a nonsense," she thought, as she dragged bryony creepers from the branches of a stubby, twisted oak and filled the barrow beside her. "After her being so dramatic yesterday on the doorstep...like it was a big emergency. She's not even here!"

Cerys resolved to stay another fifteen minutes, to show willing, and then leave if Theresa did not show. She was loathe to spend her day working for nothing. Even so, the act of weeding and setting small areas to rights a little at a time was, for Cerys, deeply absorbing and satisfying. And she had nothing else planned, did she? The big garden was already beginning to reveal some interesting secrets, too: the clouded face of a sundial strangled by ivy; the porous and mossy stone lip of a of an ancient well, dangerous and

25

dank; the date "1717" carved in sloping script on the grey face of the brickwork by the front door. Curiously, there were the remains of what Cerys assumed was the old name of the house, but this was etched on the lowest bricks on the wall nearest where the well was half-hidden still. The old-fashioned script was beautiful, slanting and sprawling, yet part of the name was missing, the stone hacked away in places as if in anger to leave only the riddle

"ELL   USE"

"Old-school vandals!" Cerys spoke aloud, running her gloved finger over the chipped and scarred letters. But why would anyone have their house name written down by the ground, she wondered? Maybe the lettering referred to the well – "Well House" would make sense, she supposed.

Standing up slowly and stiffly, Cerys suddenly realised she had been busy for nearly two hours – she had stayed much longer than intended and still no sign of Theresa. She packed her tools away and pulled off her gloves, feeling very hot and thirsty now. The front door was still open a crack. Cerys, a little vexed at herself for over-staying and quite possibly working for free, called through into the empty hallway. "I'm going now, Mrs...um...would you let Theresa know that I was here please?"

She hovered on the step, torn between waiting for acknowledgement and wanting to be away. A light, young voice piped up startlingly from the depths of the house.

"Wait! I'm here! I'm here."

Cerys looked over her shoulder instinctively; she hadn't seen anybody going past her and into the house while she was working, had she? Theresa herself then emerged from the gloom, purse in hand, beaming her slightly alarming, canine smile.

"I didn't think you were here?" Cerys said reproachfully, irritated by her self-doubt. "The other lady...she said you were out?"

26

"Oh I'm always around," Theresa waved a long-fingered hand dismissively. "My Nana gets confused. Fifty do you?"

Baffled by the odd scenario and feeling somewhat foolish, Cerys

thanked her and pocketed the notes, which were a very agreeable rate and, she decided, worth over- looking the lack of courtesy.

"See you again tomorrow, then? You'll come back?" Theresa nodded at Cerys, willing her compliance.

"Well, yes, I suppose!" Cerys replied. She had not planned to return to the garden so soon – she had not thought that far ahead in truth – but Theresa in her abrupt manner had not provided room for discussion.

She had no excuse prepared, no way of forestalling until she had considered whether she wished to go back to the strange situation there. However, as she ran a deep bath at her uncle's house that afternoon to soothe her aching limbs, she reasoned that the money was good, and the garden, albeit a heavy task, was intriguing. Cerys longed to uncover the well fully, to clear the choked beds and bring light to the treasures hidden there – purple asters and foxgloves and golden thyme all waiting to be untangled from the nettles and briars.

"One day at a time," she told herself. "See what tomorrow brings." Then she was immersed in the bliss of the warm bath, her nettle stings and scratches from thorns throbbing heartily.

*

By late evening, Cerys had concluded that the glaring, livid face she had seen at the window of the big house a few nights ago must have been Theresa's grandmother. She was, after all, entitled to look out of her own window, wasn't she? It was a little odd that she should be up and about the house in the early hours, but Cerys had to admit that a stranger such as herself walking alone in the village in the dead of night was no more peculiar. It was surely just an uncomfortable coincidence that their gaze should meet in that instance, and that Cerys should subsequently find herself working at the old lady's house. It also probably explained the woman's unfriendly demeanour upon Cerys's arrival.

After a catch- up with her mother on the 'phone ("Yes, Cerys was eating; yes, she was enjoying spending some time with Dom; yes, she was sleeping" - not a full lie, but one that was reassuring to Nancy, they both knew) Cerys did actually have a surprisingly restful night no doubt aided by the physical work of the day.

She arrived refreshed and ready to tackle the jungle that awaited her the next morning, and knocked again at the spongy, flaky front door. Cerys wanted to write an invoice and receipt for the previous day, but realised she had no details for Theresa, or even the address of the property – there was no door number to be seen, or a quaint cottage name on the gate like most of the houses in Quaintlip. Cerys was cautious of being stung in some way by the strange occupants, and wanted her work there to be recorded properly, if only to cover herself. She didn't know Theresa and her grandmother, and they didn't know her either, to be fair.

The sullen-faced lady answered the door once more, and on hearing Cerys's request she gestured ungraciously for Cerys to follow her into the dark hallway. Cerys trod slowly and patiently behind as the old woman shuffled ahead in silence.

She led Cerys into a surprisingly large, almost empty sort of reception room, facing out over the front garden. The floorboards were bare and the plaster blistered and puckered on the walls. There was a heavy-looking, dark wooden table under the big bay window, framing many ugly and overgrown houseplants. Tea chests were stacked against the walls. Cerys guessed from the damp and musty smell that they were filled with many old books.

"Still not unpacked everyfin'." The old woman nodded at the chests, looking away from Cerys. Then she pointed up at the wall and said "Them's Trayza's nayems f'ew. I dunno how to spell 'em out."

Cerys had thought perhaps the woman had brought her inside to find a piece of mail with their postcode on it, or maybe even to summon Theresa herself to come and see Cerys, and reel off contact details or whatever she needed for her invoice.

She was unprepared for this spectacle: an ancient, weathered canvas, greyish with age, hanging in a dark wooden frame. Embroidered on it in elaborate, fine script were the words:

THARAZA FAY VOLK
A.D.1893
"Blessed be the garden, from which our sorrows are mended"

The words were surrounded by embellished flowers and herbs, carefully and beautifully stitched, some of which had their names embroidered alongside or beneath them: *wolfsbane, willowherb, heartsease, mallow, foxglove, thyme.*

"Are you sure?!" Cerys faltered, somewhat rudely. Maybe the grandmother was suffering with dementia? Theresa had said that she got confused sometimes.

"Thass her nayems." The woman answered stiffly, her jaw set with stubborn certainty. "Thass Trayza's nayems. We'se all got the same." Still she looked away, to Cerys's left, never quite meeting her eyes. Cerys regained her composure and set to work writing a brief invoice at the heavy oval table, where the tangled houseplants filling the

29

window made weird tropical shadow-shapes on its surface and upon the back of Cerys's hand as she wrote.

Relieved to be back outside in the daylight and fresh air, she picked up where she had left off the day before, running barrows of weeds and other debris to the growing heap by the wall. Her mind was a little troubled as she worked, with the vague sense that all was not as it should be there. No neighbours dropping in, or people passing by even, no post van stopping by the gate. No doors or windows open even on such a bright and welcome morning, no offer of tea or a cool drink despite the warm weather. And still no sign of Theresa, and no adequate details for her except for the quirky embroidered association with a person belonging to a previous century. Cerys reasoned it must be a family name, passed on through the generations, as her grandmother had stated. It would have been common practice in days gone by. Yet from what little of the house Cerys had seen so far it looked simultaneously lived - in and derelict, as though Theresa and her grandmother had indeed just moved in, but also had somehow existed there in the gloom, unseen for silent cobwebbed decades.

Cerys packed up her things at noon – she had done three rather gruelling hours without so much as an offer of a glass tap water; she was hot and scratchy from brambles and she needed the loo. Nobody answered this time when she knocked half-heartedly to say goodbye so she pushed her paper invoice under the door and returned to her uncle's house feeling a little dispirited.

Uncle Dom bought them fish and chips that evening. They ate sitting on the stone steps of his back garden, which was really just a small thin slice of courtyard, elegantly walled on all three sides with flint draped in ivy. They balanced their plates on their knees, ketchup and vinegar bottles and cans of cold Coke at their feet.

Cerys felt slightly guilty as they chatted and ate – she had been staying at her uncle's home for a week now and had not yet even looked at his garden, much less considered what she was able to do to improve it. He had not asked her yet, and at his own admission he did not use the garden very much, but perhaps that was due to its neglected state, and his lack of garden knowledge and time to make it a more aesthetically pleasing place to sit.

Once they had finished eating, Cerys began to lug a few of the tired- looking terracotta tubs around, bringing them into groups of three and five, instead of their former random scattered positions. They all had mostly stringy grass and moss growing out of them, and hosts of crusty snails on the sides which had faced the shade.

"They all need emptying," Cerys said, from where she knelt in the dust. "And fresh compost, for starters. They look like they've not been touched for years. But something climbing could look nice by this wall here? Maybe a clematis? It would make a nice feature of the wall, and draw the eye upwards once it's grown a bit."

Uncle Dom nodded, head to one side, considering. He was beginning to imagine the garden with colour and depth, instead of the grey outside space he had, up until now, largely ignored. Having discussed some more ideas and agreed that a trip to the nearest plant nursery would be in order, Cerys and Dom retired to their rooms; he to catch up on work emails and the news headlines, and she to read, restlessly, her mind still turning over the strange set-up at her new place of work.

As the day began to turn towards evening and the sky became luminous, with clouds the colour of bloodshot pink roses, there was a knock at the front door. Cerys heard her uncle's footsteps as he thudded barefoot downstairs to answer. She could tell from the tone of his voice that something of concern had happened.

31

Cerys sat and waited, on a stair midway down. Eventually her uncle closed the door and said; "Mrs Devin had a fall last night." He nodded in the direction of his neighbour's house : the elderly lady to whom he had introduced Cerys when she first arrived in Quaintlip.

"She's still in hospital; that was her daughter, Elaine here just now. She's come up from London. She asked if we could mind the dog for a few days, until they know when Mrs D. might be back on her feet again?"

"Poor Mrs Devin!" said Cerys. "And poor Flowers. He must be distraught."

"Indeed," Dom agreed. It was rare that he actually saw his neighbour; but when he did, the little dog was always at her side.

"Elaine has him with her today, but she's got young kids at home and she's got to get back tonight. They're in a third floor flat, so it's not practical to take the dog back there."

Dom was due to be away working again that weekend, so it was agreed that Cerys would take Flowers out during the day, and pop in to feed him and let him out before bedtime. He gave her the key to Mrs Devin's house, tucked in to an envelope by her daughter. It would be nice, Dom thought, for Cerys to have a little company in his absence. He prayed fleetingly that she would make a friend or two in the village during her stay with him: someone to have fun with. He also prayed, before he fell asleep that night, for her well-being over the coming weekend – that she would not look as drawn and fearful as she had on his last return home – and that she would sleep soundly and find some peace in her solitude.

Cerys's thoughts as she lay in bed before drifting off into unquiet dreams were not peaceful at all. A question had burst into her consciousness and she could not rid herself of it. Her contact cards had only her name and mobile number on them, and "Garden Maintenance." How had Theresa known where to find her the day she'd come to ask -demand - Cerys's help? How had she known where she was staying? To this question Cerys had no answer.

*

Uncle Dom left at six the following morning, and Cerys was up soon after. She was on edge: it had been a disturbed night, during which she had dreamed of grey and black birds flapping into her peripheral vision and then retreating as she turned her head to see them. This was replaced by a recurring dream Cerys had experienced many times of angelic, crystalline snowflakes which Cerys held in her open hands and on her tongue but which refused to melt, both confusing and delighting her, as always. She was almost relieved to wake so early. Also, she was conscious of Flowers the dog, alone next door and perhaps desperately needing to go outside.

After a quick coffee and toast she tied her hair up into a long ponytail, washed, and pulled on blue jeans, yellow hooded top and faded grey high-tops, and took the key to Mrs Devin's house out of its envelope.

Flowers, curled up in his slightly smelly bed since the previous evening and bereft of his beloved owner, blinked glumly up at Cerys in the pale early morning light.

"Hello mate!" she greeted him gently, stooping to caress his wrinkled head. Flowers was a hybrid; an unattractive mix of pug and perhaps Staffordshire bull terrier, chestnut brown in colour with black rings around his bulbous eyes and an overshot bottom jaw. It made his little teeth poke up so that his upper lips rested permanently on their points. Cerys could not help but smile.

"Get you some breakfast shall we?"

Flowers did not have much appetite, which Cerys suspected to be due to him pining for his owner. They

33

headed out into a quiet Saturday morning, Cerys enjoying the comforting feeling of the dog at her side, and his lead in her hand.

She decided to walk to the end of the high street, and from there maybe choose the footpath that led up the hill to St Mary's Church, in order to look about the old graveyard there. Cerys had always felt an affinity with graveyards (" A *morbid* fascination!" her mum laughingly referred to it). She was intrigued by old tombstones and their engravings, and the gargoyles and carvings that could be found in church architecture.

Cerys also thought that, if she was passing Theresa's house, that she might catch either her or her grandmother by chance , as an opportunity to casually remind them of the invoice she had left yesterday and the work she had done which had thus far not even been acknowledged.

There were no signs of life at the house, however – it was just as silent and still as when Cerys had first laid eyes upon it. Cerys modestly noted the progress made by her two mornings' hard work outside. It was easier to see the difference from the road than from within the garden boundaries. The lines of the pathway and beds were beginning to take shape again, and there were a healthy amount of cuttings and weeds built up on the rubbish heap, ready to burn when it dried out enough.

Cerys turned to walk the steep and narrow lane up to the church. The creamy white blur of hawthorn blossom arched and met overhead, enclosing the lane in a fairytale tunnel of fragrance, so that Cerys felt quite dazzled by the time that she reached the lych-gate at the top of the hill. It was as if she were back in her dream of the snowflakes which refused to melt, sparkling and piling higher and higher, surreal and beautiful. Immersed in her reverie, Cerys was startled to see a tall black figure, back to her, hunched in the shade of the oak arch.

34

The figure turned to face Cerys then, and she saw that it was Theresa, clad in skinny black jeans, long black shirt almost reaching to her knees, with her lank, dark hair hanging loose over her stooped shoulders.

"You'se got company!" Theresa greeted her, gesturing towards Flowers, panting at Cerys's feet after the steady ascent. Theresa's solemn face transformed suddenly with her enormous hungry grin, her eyes sparkling with what seemed to be real pleasure at seeing Cerys and the little dog.

"Hi," replied Cerys. "He's not mine." Then she added, although it was rather obvious, but she was unprepared for conversation; "I'm walking him."

"Oh. Join you?" Theresa asked, and did not really ask at all. She nodded Cerys's acquiescence without waiting for her answer and stepped in with Cerys as they continued on through the graveyard.

"Grand job yesterday by the way," Theresa said, delving into her jeans pocket and drawing out flattened notes. "Fifty pound again?"

Cerys took the notes, feeling a little uneasy. "She must have seen me walking past the house?" she thought. But Theresa had reached the lych-gate before Cerys, and couldn't have passed her.

"Funny that she had the exact amount of money on her too," Cerys wondered silently as they strolled, their footsteps matching each others' on the soft carpet of grass.

Theresa poked around the tilting and weathered tombstones as though she were at a greengrocers choosing apples, saying conversationally to nobody in particular; "This 'un was a hardy old thing." Then, crouched low to the mossy face of another crumbling stone, "Rotten to the core they was – bad blood in that family." Cerys followed at a reasonable distance, both intrigued at her companion's animated behaviour and slightly irritated that she was now

35

part of someone else's walk, and no longer on her own peaceful outing.

Cerys drew closer to Theresa as she knelt at a mossy weather-beaten rock in the long grass, and overheard her mutter quietly at the ground: "Thought you were so clever...ha. I saw you for what *you* was. Got what you 'ad comin' by all the elements, din't you!" It was as if Theresa had forgotten she had company at all and was actively immersed in another world entirely.

Cerys, waiting awkwardly for Theresa to realise she was more or less beside her, became vaguely aware of a man in her peripheral vision, standing some way off, watching them. Perhaps he was visiting a grave, Cerys thought, or perhaps he is lost. She and Theresa rounded the East wall of the church, the centuries-old mortar breathing coolness over them in their close proximity. Flowers stopped to relieve himself heavily at Cerys's feet. She found a bag with which to pick it up, Theresa looking on with distaste.

As Cerys rose from scooping up Flower's mess one-handed, she saw that the man, who had been some distance from them, was now suddenly very much in front of she and Theresa, just a few feet away in fact. He was a man of heavy build, and tall with it, perhaps in his late fifties and he was wearing a long oilskin coat which struck Cerys as odd for the time of year and the glorious weather. This thought was swiftly followed by the realisation that he had dropped his trousers and was busy manipulating his manhood and smiling directly at the two women, his mouth open and his jaw working with pleasure.

Cerys and Theresa stood staring in surprise, momentarily frozen to the spot. There was no social etiquette to deal with this. The man, still leering, took a step forward then, and without thought Cerys reached back her strong right arm and launched the untied bag containing

36

Flower's stinking gift at the man's stupidly smiling face. By luck, the bag landed openly with a soft *thwack* on his gaping mouth. His face fell instantly - the leering mask turned upside down from comedy to tragedy- and his hand fell limply to his side.

Cerys and Theresa burst into explosive, howling laughter and turned and ran out of the graveyard, back down the steep lane, stumbling and sliding on the chalky gravel as they fled wild-eyed and cackling, grasping for each other's elbows as they fought to stay on their feet the faster their descent unraveled. Flowers barked as he ran alongside the two women, their sudden outburst triggering old instincts long-forgotten during his sedate later years with Mrs Devin.

They came to a sliding halt at the bottom of the hill, and leaned against trees, gasping for breath and still laughing.

"That was brilliant!" Theresa exclaimed, her sweaty face turned towards Cerys. "Fucking brilliant shot!"

"I don't know where it came from!" Cerys answered truthfully, raking her hands through her hair, away from her face. "I just did it without thinking." Her legs were beginning to feel a little shaky now.

"The dirty beast." Theresa said, glaring up the hill towards the church. "Got what he deserved. Will you come back to the house for a drink?"

Cerys nodded: a cold drink and somewhere safe to sit for a few moments sounded favourable. "That would be great," she said, feeling herself warming to Theresa suddenly, as she opened her rickety front gate for Cerys and they hurried, still giggling, to Theresa's front door.

*

It was six-thirty of that same evening and, almost a hundred miles away, Cerys's mother Nancy was due to start

37

the second night shift of her usual five in a row at the hospital at eight.

"Saturday night *and* a full moon," she had sighed, upon waking late in the afternoon. The flat seemed emptier that evening, her daughter's absence more keenly felt to her mother, with the prospect of a daunting shift ahead. Weekends were always busier at work, of course, but night shift on a full moon was the worst, it was commonly agreed amongst most of her colleagues. This was not a superstition-driven and neurotic concept, but an undeniable, dreary fact. The full moon – especially one that happened to fall on a weekend- historically brought with it an increase in violence on the streets, and a crescendo of domestic abuse cases, leading to more injuries for A and E to process. People suffering from mental health crisis often seemed to reach their point of breakdown during this short period and addicts over-consumed with greater fervour. Combined with the traditional extra weight of Saturday night booze-related accidents and inflictions, it was likely to be a taxing night ahead.

Nancy ate cereal and drank tea, accustomed after many years of working unsociable hours to waking with the daylight dwindling and breakfasting whilst watching the evening news. This evening she struggled to shake off a sense of unease; a foreboding that cloaked itself around her like a damp fog. She showered and dressed in her uniform, sternly telling her own reflection in the bedroom mirror to get a grip, and focus on the night ahead.

Nancy resolved to ring Cerys at seven-fifteen. It would help to put her mind at ease to hear her daughter's voice, even from so far away, and to go to whatever lay ahead at the hospital that night with the comfort of knowing that Cerys, her most precious person in the whole world, was safely occupied at Dom's place, at possibly the quietest rural location imaginable.

38

Her feeling of undefined anxiety increased tenfold when, at quarter past seven, Cerys's phone simply rang and rang. She tried calling Dom, whose number went straight to voicemail: of course, she remembered – he was working away again weekend. She tried Cerys again, to no avail. She would have to try again later, if she was able to steal a five minute break to make the call. She reminded herself that Cerys was seventeen now, really an adult in all but law, and that she should relinquish her grip somewhat, for her own well-being as well as her daughter's.

But still, it was unlike Cerys not even send her mother a text to say she was busy, or she was out, and that she would call later. And where indeed would she be if not at her uncle's house? Quaintlip was hardly a party destination. Cerys's phone rang out for a third time: what if she'd fallen down the stairs, or been knocked over by a car into a ditch, or…Nancy was both cross and troubled now, and conscious that if she didn't hurry she would be late to work, a thing she hated. She stuffed her phone and charger into her bag and had just reached the door to their flat, keys in hand, when her phone started to vibrate. She emptied the bag fully on the hall carpet in her rush to find the phone. Cerys's photo lit up the screen.

"Mum? Mum!" her voice sounded bubbly and bright.

"Cerys? Are you ok? I was getting worried darling!" Nancy juggled keys and phone at the front door as she locked up: she would be terribly late now if she stopped to chat.

"I'm ok, Mum!" Cerys answered, sounding rather breathless, Nancy thought. "I was at a…a friend's house. I've been doing her garden for her."

"Oh, who's that then, darling?" Nancy frowned: irrationally, her sense of unease was flooding back like bile.

"She's a…well, I don't know what she is, actually." And Cerys dissolved into sniggering laughter.

39

Nancy put her hand on the metal rail of the walkway that lead to the stairs, and paused for a moment, closing her eyes briefly.

"Cerys, have you been drinking, love?" she asked. "The doctor said you shouldn't, not with the tablets you're taking."

"I'm fine, Mum," came the giggly reply. "Oh Mum, we got flashed at. Up by the church here. It was the funniest thing – you should have been there!" Cerys broke up with laughter again, the phone line cutting in and out. Nancy didn't recall the signal being that bad at her brother's place – Cerys sounded like she was in a hailstorm, her voice fragmented and pitted with static.

"I've got to get to work, darling, I'm running late now. I'll call you later, ok? Wherever you are the signal's terrible – I can't hear you very well." Nancy was fully annoyed now, and possibly even more worried than she had been before Cerys had returned her missed calls.

"You really should have gone to the police, love, not gone drinking. What's your friend's name, anyway? Does Dom know her?"

"Nobody knows her, Mum," came the blurry reply, and a long sigh like the wind through bare winter trees, which Nancy was not sure came from Cerys or the poor phone connection.

"I'm going to lie down now, Mum. Love you."

The line went dead.

*

Cerys awoke much later that night with a dry mouth and a head full of fog. She had apparently not moved in several hours, she discovered: her limbs were stiff and cold and her head sunken deep into the squashy velvet cushion on Uncle Dom's sofa. The front room was dark and cool – the

40

curtains had been drawn shut all day and the house was still and silent. It took Cerys a great effort to sit upright.

"What were we drinking?" She asked wretchedly of the emptiness surrounding her. She remembered the walk up to the church, the trouser-less, leering man braced with his feet apart amongst the gravestones, running down the hill to Theresa's house – the both of them shrieking with laughter – Flowers leaping and barking alongside them. Flowers; where was he? Cerys had a cloudy recollection of improvising a clumsy bed for him out of tea towels and a sheepskin coat. With huge relief she found the dog curled up in a tight circle on the makeshift bed under the kitchen table.

She remembered sharing something cold and fizzy and bitter to drink in Theresa's kitchen: there was an Aga in there, and it had been very warm, indoors as well as out. They went into the back garden (as much as it could be called a garden) to cool off, and sat beside a stagnant pond where baby frogs crawled in the long grass at the edges. Theresa and Cerys had talked and talked as if they had been waiting to meet each other all their lives.

When Cerys described her night-time terrors and explained why she had come to stay in Quaintlip for the summer, Theresa had, miraculously, understood straight away. Cerys felt no need to convince Theresa of her own sanity, or validate her fear in some way. Theresa accepted and believed Cerys's predicament, as easily as though Cerys were telling her that she didn't like heights, or had a phobia about spiders.

Moreover, Theresa said she knew of ways to combat that kind of bad spirit, she said, and that she was experienced in dealing with them. The spirit had attached itself to Cerys, like a parasite, and was thriving in her misery. It was the first time that Cerys had been able to make some sense of her problem, even if the explanation

41

was outlandish, and something of which she had very little knowledge. So far, Theresa was the only person Cerys had confided in who could offer her any convincing reassurance that things would get better.

"I can help you deal with that," Theresa had said, nodding, when Cerys described the immense pressure she often felt in the air in her room when she was experiencing a bad night. "And something you'se can take before bed to help you sleep...it's home-made, all natural, like?"

Cerys's memory of the rest of the long afternoon was blurry after that – the hours had seemed to rocket past. They downed more of the earthy drink – lots more – Cerys was *so* thirsty. "From the garden," Theresa had winked and grinned, her black eyes sparkling, when Cerys asked where it came from. Eventually, she needed to use the toilet – she was in such earnest conversation with Theresa that she had failed to notice how badly she needed to go. Theresa pointed her up the stairs to the bathroom on the right of a long, bare landing. All the other doors were shut: Cerys wondered briefly where Theresa's grandmother was and if she were asleep in one of the closed rooms. She must be very deaf, Cerys reasoned, not to have stirred with us two in the house, laughing and talking and crashing bottles and glasses about downstairs.

Cerys vaguely recalled black and white tiles in the ancient bathroom, and copper pipework on the walls, and just a chipped green and pink-flowered jug and a large, shallow bowl on a wooden mount where the sink might usually be. Cerys's legs felt as if they belonged to somebody else: they were suddenly far too long and unmanageable, like those of a new-born foal or a baby giraffe, she balanced precariously on them.

Her head spinning a little by now, and grown suddenly weary, Cerys remembered leaving the cool bathroom where she swayed at the top of the stairs, gripping the bannister, and observed another tapestry canvas, similar to the one in the reception room below. It was hung above the stairwell, heavily cobwebbed in the gloom.

Cerys remembered suddenly that she had been compelled to take a photo of the tapestry with the last of her dying phone battery: perhaps because at the time it hurt her head to try and decipher the intricate lettering, and perhaps because she was acting outside of her normal waking world on this foggy-headed, euphoric afternoon. She was not entirely sure what had made her take the picture, but here in the dark of Uncle Dom's kitchen, kneeling next to the mournful Flowers on his strange new bed, she plugged in her long-dead phone and revived the battery enough to open up her photo gallery.

There she saw the shadowy canvas, and zoomed in close to read the spidery, slanting script:

"WE HEAL, AND CURSE, AND ARE CURSED AGAIN."

Below this were two crescent moons, back to back, so that they looked like a dainty pair of horns and what looked like a sprig of rosemary, violet- blue flowers exquisitely detailed between them.

Cerys stared, baffled, at the riddle, which seemed an odd sort of a nonsense to her. "But what a weird thing to have hanging on your wall?" she wondered. "Unless it was there already when they moved in?" It had been a weird day altogether though, Cerys smiled. But a good one. She hadn't talked or laughed so much in months. So what if Theresa and her gran had some odd stuff up on their walls? Cerys herself was just beginning to open up to some strange new concepts – things that she had not even considered before yesterday afternoon – things which Cerys knew some people would certainly label as weird and/or ridiculous. Theresa had promised to be able to help her, and that was more than any doctor or pills had managed yet.

43

Cerys filled a cereal bowl with water for Flowers, who had buried his nose once more in sheepskin. She climbed the stairs to her room and crawled gratefully under the duvet, her phone battery dead once more and her skull aching. She could think only of sleep, and morning, when she would see if Theresa would be free to meet up again, to go back to her house again, or to walk Flowers with her. Anything, as long as they could see each other, and continue the intoxicating conversation.

Cerys woke at noon on Sunday, and plugged in her phone to find many missed calls from her mother, plus several from Uncle Dom, too. She had the uncomfortable realisation that she actually felt more guilty about her uncle's genuine concern than her mother's. Under normal circumstances, he did not have to worry about anyone else, not seriously, and he was content with his life choices. Now she, Cerys had overlooked this - not deliberately, but through her own thoughtlessness – and had taken that choice away. He hadn't asked for her to come and stay in his quiet, peaceful home, after all, and so far Cerys felt she had brought nothing but drama and worry to his door.

After letting Flowers out into the tiny garden, feeding him and tidying his heap of coat and towels away (which also stung her conscience mightily- the poor hound also never had a choice in the events of the previous evening and had been, until yesterday, a creature used to a sensible routine) Cerys made coffee and embarked upon the task of ringing both her mother and uncle to apologise, and to try and placate their worry.

"It was just a bit out of character, Ces,"said a rushed-sounding Dom at work, against a lot of background voices. He was clearly very busy, which made the call feel worse somehow. "That was what worried us the most. And with everything else that's going on with you...we didn't know what was happening."

"I'm really sorry," said Cerys, meaning it.

"We'll catch up when I get back," said Dom. "I've got to get off the phone now...message me later, Ok? And *eat* something, something healthy!"

Her mother sounded tired, and hurt.

"I don't mind that you were out, Love. I'm happy that you've made a friend there. It's just that I was always able to reach you before, you know? To know that you were safe, wherever you were."

"I'm sorry, Mum. It won't happen again." The irony, Cerys thought, being that she had not felt "safe" over the past year whilst in her own room, in their flat, where both her mum and anybody else who was at all concerned knew exactly where she was, every night.

She walked with Flowers down to the village shop/café, where she bought a treacle tart, and some potted herbs from the plant stand outside , as a peace offering for Uncle Dom. She deliberately avoided north end of the high street, her common sense telling her that a second lost afternoon with Theresa would not be advisable so soon. Her soul ached with wanting very badly to be in Theresa's strange company again, to be allowed in to her world and gifted with her astonishing, Cheshire-cat grin. But Cerys could not bear the thought of seeing disapproval and suspicion in Uncle Dom's eyes every time she mentioned Theresa's name from now on. He didn't know Theresa, Cerys understood that. But she hated the idea that he might already think poorly of her. It was not Theresa's fault that Cerys had gone A.W.O.L., was it? She was responsible for her own actions, nobody else.

Cerys returned Flowers back to his own home, filled his water bowl, and fed him biscuits. She assured him in gentle tones that she would be back later to see him, while he crunched his food laboriously, little pieces dropping from the gaps in his teeth on to the linoleum floor. Cerys left him hunched up gratefully in his own bed, locked Mrs Devin's front door and returned to Uncle Dom's house.

Cerys busied herself with planting the herbs in a chipped and mossy terracotta urn by the back step. She was watering them in carefully when she heard a loud knocking at the front door. "Elaine," she thought, wiping her hands on her jeans as she stood up. "Perhaps she needs the key back."

Cerys was surprised and delighted to see instead the gawky figure of Theresa, her foot upon the doorstep in the same expectant stance that had so irritated Cerys less than a week ago.

"Somethin' for you!" Theresa announced in her usual abrupt manner. Cerys hesitated, unsure of the etiquette of inviting a stranger in to her uncle's house in his absence. Especially Theresa. Cerys's pleasure at seeing her turned swiftly to guiltily wondering whether Dom might return home unexpectedly, and catch her there, adding salt to the very recent wound. Then Theresa's face suddenly lit up with her wide, heart-stopping grin and she reached forward and squeezed Cerys's arm as if to pull her into a hug. Cerys's uncertainty was dispelled instantly – Theresa was here! She allowed herself to reach forward in reciprocation but she must have misjudged the moment for Theresa merely side-stepped her through the open door and into the kitchen.

"This'll help you sleep." Theresa said, depositing a sturdy brown glass bottle upon the cluttered pine table. Cerys glanced dubiously at it. The bottle was about three inches high, with a cork stopper in the top, and no label.

"Made it myself," Theresa nodded towards the bottle. "All natural, from the garden, like."

46

"From the garden?!" thought Cerys, tenderly amused. "That big jungle of nettles and blackthorn and God knows what else?"

"And.." Theresa paused, with some air of drama, then continued " I need to do a Cleanse of the 'ouse. And there's this. You'se can 'ang it up in your bedrum, for protection. Or wear it. 'Tis the same effect."

She placed something lightly around Cerys's neck; something that felt like soft leather, only warm and supple as a length of living skin. A small black pendant hung from it, like an arrow-head, Cerys thought, which weighed surprisingly heavily around her slender throat.

"Thanks," Cerys said, touching the pendant tip, feeling the grainy, brittle surface. "What was the other thing…the "cleanse"? How does that work?"

"Drives bad spirits out," Theresa answered, her eyes sparkling like jet. "I asks them politely to leave. And if they be stubborn, I gets stronger with them. They don't like it when I call them out."

A thought manifested itself, sly and uncomfortable, like indigestion, at the back of Cerys's mind. *She sounds like she's excited about the whole thing."* As if it were nothing to be afraid of – a game to be played. Cerys supposed that it was reassuring that Theresa was confident in her ability to do whatever it was she had planned in order to help Cerys. She was deeply grateful that Theresa cared enough to try but Cerys could not ignore a growing sense of alarm. She would have liked to sit down and talk it through with Theresa over a drink, and discuss the way forward. She wasn't really prepared, mentally or physically, for this kind of instant warfare.

"Do you… can we hang fire, just wait a few minutes?" Cerys asked, putting a hand out gently to touch Theresa's sleeve. She didn't want her to be offended, or worse, to lose patience with Cerys's naivety and retract her offer. But

47

Theresa was already pushing past her, moving purposefully from room to room in Uncle Dom's little house, her hands held up in front of her face as if to protect her eyes.

Theresa spoke in low, insistent tones, words which Cerys did not fully hear or understand – perhaps another language altogether, she thought, a spiritual language, like speaking in tongues. Theresa was fully absorbed in her task, oblivious to Cerys treading anxiously behind her.

Theresa made her way upstairs without pausing to ask permission – something that Cerys would never do in a strange house. She stood for a long while in Cerys's box room, her incantations unbroken and becoming louder in there, surrounded by Cerys's crumpled clothes and books and unmade bed.

Cerys felt a prickling of her skin, on her scalp and upper arms. The familiar malevolent atmosphere was descending upon the room, the kind she associated with the onset of a very bad night's fearful wakefulness. It was the signal for Cerys that whatever entity or elemental force it was that tormented her so frequently had arrived.

She felt the urge to break into Theresa's relentless, mysterious monologue, wanting desperately to tell her "Stop, this is too much, this *thing* is not meant to be here in daylight, it doesn't belong here, not now!!" For if "it" could be summoned like this, during a bright afternoon, then there would be no respite for Cerys, ever. And what if Theresa was not able now to rid them of it, whatever "it" was? But her words faltered as Theresa chanted on, her eyes closed, Cerys's discomfort unheeded as she hung back, tearing the ragged skin around her fingernails with her teeth as she watched.

When Theresa moved on to stand at Uncle Dom's bedroom door, the charge in the atmosphere became almost unbearably intense, and a cry escaped Cerys suddenly.

"No, you can't go in there!"

48

She stepped forward without thinking what she was doing, and placed herself between Theresa and the open doorway. Theresa opened her eyes and lowered her hands slowly.

"It's my uncle's room." Cerys said quietly, firmly. " It's private."

"Won't work if I don't do the 'ole 'ouse." Theresa said, in a sulky voice, a child interrupted at play. She leant forward as if to push past Cerys.

"No," said Cerys. "I'm really sorry … I'm grateful for all…this…I really am, but I can't let you in there."

Theresa shrugged, her concentration lost, and Cerys felt the sinister grip in the air loosen.

"Think on it." Theresa said. "I can always come back." She sloped down the staircase, saying over her shoulder "You will come back tomorrow – carry on in the garden, like? Lots more to do. Gran will be expecting you." As always with Theresa, it was a statement rather than a question. Cerys let a long, quiet breath of tension escape her, hoping that Theresa would not notice. Glad that the uncomfortable episode was over, she answered her brightly.

"Of course, I'll see you then." She had the strong sensation of danger having been averted, as though she had stepped out on to a busy road without thinking and just pulled herself back in time on to the kerb before a lorry floored her. Or perhaps, a small voice told Cerys, she was simply relieved that Theresa was not angry with her for halting the slightly fevered scene in the house.

Still hungover from the previous lost and hazy day, and shaky from the disturbing event upstairs in her uncle's house, Cerys sat numbly for a short while at the kitchen table after Theresa left. She tried to place the scenes of the past few days in some kind of order in her mind, to rationalise them, but the images and information swam round and round in her head like fish in an aquarium. They slipped in and out of her tired mind's grasp, appearing with clarity one moment and disappearing into darkness the next.

She still sensed that unpleasant energy lingering overhead, and knew that if she ventured up the staircase her skin would crawl, and she would find no respite in her room.

Eventually, she dragged herself to the sofa in the living room where she curled up with her knees to her chest and closed her weary eyes. She touched the amulet at her throat with her fingertips, anxiously hoping that Theresa was not annoyed with her now, and did not think her a child. She just felt that it would have been very wrong to allow her to enter Uncle Dom's bedroom – his safe and peaceful space – with that dreadful feeling in the atmosphere. Cerys's instincts had warned her that to do so would somehow grant the awful energy, spirit, or whatever it was, access to him. That, she felt, would have been unforgivable.

It was almost four o'clock, and Cerys would need to take the lovely Flowers out soon. "Ten minutes," she told herself. "I'll go in ten minutes."

She was asleep.

*

"Home!" Uncle Dom announced happily later that evening, hauling a small suitcase on wheels noisily across the kitchen floor tiles. Cerys had stirred at the rattle of the key in the lock and leaned through the living room doorway, long hair swinging over one shoulder.

"Welcome back!" she greeted him. Dom flicked on the bright overhead light.

"Ooh…yowch. Hangover?!" He feigned a grimace, noting his niece's pale face and panda-circles of shadow around her eyes.

"Something like that," Cerys blinked against the bright light, smiling sheepishly, and a sudden impulsion made her hug him with brief intensity. She was surprised in that moment at how gladdened her heart was to see him. She took pleasure in making tea and presenting her uncle with the apologetic treacle tart, which they ate from plates balanced on their laps in the front room as the last of the day's light left the sky.

They shared bits of news, mostly about Dom's work: his funny colleagues, and a heated row amongst them over who took all the plastic dessert glasses from the mobile canteen back to their trailer for drinks, meaning the rest of the hard-working crew had to eat Eton mess out of vending-machine cups. "I mean, it was the one thing, *the one thing*, we were looking forward to after Danish pastries ran out on the second morning! Ruined, it was, slopping it out of those nasty cups like tepid soup."

They visited Flowers next door together, switching on timer lamps and lighting the wood-burner to keep the chill off the empty house overnight, and returned home.

"You really worried your mum you know," Uncle Dom scolded Cerys casually, as they sat amongst the clutter of the kitchen table for a last mug of tea before bed.

"I know," Cerys nodded. She had, of course, expected this conversation at some stage of the evening. "I did call her today. We *discussed*. I think she's OK now."

"I'd love to see what you've been doing in that garden," Dom continued lightly. "Must be transforming the place. Perhaps I could walk up with Flowers tomorrow while you're working there and be nosy? Catch a sneaky look at the place too?" He added with a wink.

"*He's checking up on me,*" Cerys thought. "*Wants to meet Theresa, see if she's a crackhead or something.*"

"Of course!" she answered brightly. (*"Change the subject, Cerys!"*) "Have you heard any more news about Mrs Devin? How is she?"

"Ah, Elaine rang me yesterday. It was mid-take. I had to call her back pretty late. But Mrs D. is coming back on Tuesday apparently. Bed-rest for at least another fortnight, and she'll have carers coming in to help her. So we'll still be on dog-walking duties for a bit longer- is that ok with you?"

"It's no problem at all." Cerys said, meaning it. "I like him. It's good for me too, I think, walking him and all."

Cerys went to her room early that evening, the sky still holding a tranquil peach glow. She read. She drank a lot of water. She wanted to be well-rested and fresh for the following morning's work in the garden. Whatever the peculiar circumstances were, the money was favourable and Cerys hated to leave a job unfinished. She told herself that maybe she had been a little neurotic earlier that day, when Theresa had visited, and had made too much of the situation. Theresa was trying to help her after all, and understood Cerys in a way that she had not experienced before she came to Quaintlip. More than anything, Cerys hoped with all her heart to be able to spend time with Theresa again, with more irreverent laughter, exchanges of confidences and hours that sped by in deep conversation.

Sleep, however, did not come easily to Cerys that night. Even with the daylight still lingering as a razor-edge of electric blue on the horizon, she could sense the crackle of unease in the stuffy air of her tiny room, making it seem even smaller and more claustrophobic as she lay in the single bed staring up at the ceiling.

It was an insidious, creeping sensation that Cerys imagined was akin to being followed in the dark, and being too afraid to turn around for fear of who - or what - was lurking in the shadows.

She would not close her eyes for more than brief moments during this sort of long night. She could not explain why but to her it seemed that to lose herself to sleep would leave her exposed and vulnerable to attack from whatever it was that tormented her so. To fall asleep in the presence of the enemy would be to lose the battle entirely.

Cerys was not convinced of the existence of ghosts, as such – not in the sense of dead people's bodily forms floating around and carrying out earthly activities as though they had never died and been buried or cremated. But she had no explanation for this undefined presence which sought her out nocturnally.

She had realised early on that it was not an option to call her friends or her mother for comfort or reassurance during these hateful times. She instinctively felt that if she were to reach out to them whilst she was under the influence of the terror she would somehow transfer it's attentions to them, like a contagion increasing it's number. She did not wish to draw her loved ones into her nightmare, hoping only that eventually it would tire of her and leave her be.

Cerys was also acutely aware that her dilemma exhibited signs of her having mental health issues. She realised that people would be completely justified to reach that conclusion under the circumstances, but that would not make it true. These things determined her decision not to divulge the full story of what was troubling her to those she loved most. Thus the circle of fear and secrecy had been drawn tight around her until she met Theresa. Her hopes had been raised. But now, in the tiny bedroom, Cerys did not feel that the "cleansing" of the house had been a success at all – the cleansing of what, exactly, she was still not sure. Perhaps, she thought, the problem was within herself after all.

Cerys gripped the tooth-like amulet around her neck and waited in the unkind glare of the ceiling light until dawn, when she finally felt able to rest her eyes safely. She decided against sampling the home-made remedy in the small brown bottle, although she felt guilty about it, as though she were letting Theresa down. Her mum was right though – she should be careful about what she mixed with the sleeping tablets she had been prescribed. She took them sporadically, forgetting or ignoring them some evenings. They would work for a few hours sometimes when she was really desperate. But mostly the fear of falling asleep was greater than the physical need. Cerys was still, however, reasonably cautious of their unknown effects especially when combined with a mystery homeopathic medicine.

Monday morning began sorrowfully overcast, with the metallic scent of rain weighing heavily in the air. Dom, passing his niece's closed bedroom door at ten-thirty, noted the artificial light escaping the door frame. He understood this to mean that she had stayed up all night, and eventually slept with the light on, and did not want to wake her.

"Weather's changed anyway," he told himself as he made his way downstairs to make tea. "Be raining heavy within the hour, she'll not be working outside in that."

He was on a day off, he could see to Flowers. The forecast was due to improve by the end of the week. Cerys could go back to that place then, if she's up to it, Dom reasoned. At eleven, when Cerys had still not surfaced, Dom decided to take lonely Flowers for a walk before the rain set in. They would stroll up the high street and he could knock at the strange house to let them know that Cerys would staying at home today, but would return in a couple of days.

Cerys had mentioned that her new friend and her grandmother did not have a landline. Not many people bothered now, Dom supposed, but he did find it odd that neither of them had a mobile number - especially the younger woman. "Maybe they're trying to be off-grid," he thought. "Or maybe they just don't like to give their number out. It's not a crime, I guess."

Flowers greeted Dom with hand-licking and waited, tail waving slowly, by Mrs Devin's front door for Dom to find his collar and lead. They made their way up the high street as the first light drops of rain fell and speckled the dusty tarmac. The air seemed bound to Dom, striding comfortably out on long, lean legs. It felt somehow charged with expectation; the cool vapour resting on his face and hair, awaiting the downpour which promised to hiss and spray as it hit the road and the traffic which would pass through Quaintlip later that day.

Dom reached the last house at the end of the village and his sharp eyes observed discreetly the peeling gate, the crumbling flint wall, the twisted, stubby oak and the broken slabs on the pathway. He could see where Cerys had been working hard to free the slabs of the worst of the weeds, and in doing so she had granted access to the front door, with dense nettles and wildflowers reaching for the sun on either side of the recently-cleared, narrow path. Dom raised his elbows to avoid being stung as he approached the front door.

He knocked, waited, knocked again. He took a step back and gazed up at the building. The windows were all closed up tight, despite the recent spell of pleasant warm weather. In fact they did not look like they had been opened for many years. Tendrils of ivy and vines snaked across their filthy panes and networks of ancient cobwebs upon cobwebs nestled in the wooden frames, undisturbed for a very long time.

Dom's curiosity piqued: perhaps, he thought, the new occupants did not use the front aspect of the house – some people chose to make the rear of their homes the main entrance, especially in proximity to a busy road such as Quaintlip's main thoroughfare.

"I wouldn't want to look out on that view either," Dom thought, his gaze returning to the jungle of weeds and the towering leylandii hedge, appearing almost black in the subdued atmosphere of impending rain. "They must be living in that monster's shadow all the time in the house." A shiver took hold of him abruptly, the damp air clammy on his face. Flowers whined softly.

"Goose walking over my grave!" Dom said to nobody. "I'll just stick my head round the back quickly, just in case. The old lady might not have heard me knocking. Try them one more time. C'Mon, Pup."

He tugged Flowers' thin lead gently, and pushed open the antiquated iron gate at the side of the building. Still no sign of anyone being at home there; no window ajar, no television or radio blare, no boots by the back door, no light on in the house. A blanket of creepers and wild white roses sprawled upwards across the brickwork and ugly, overgrown houseplants dominated the grimy windows from within.

Flowers pulled unhappily at his lead and the rain was becoming heavier. Dom, feeling distinctly uncomfortable in the presence of the neglected house, was glad to leave the place. They walked hastily back with their heads bowed against the downpour, beneath the metal clouds that breached the daylight and matched Dom's thoughts as they hurried home.

Cerys woke at noon, feeling hot and groggy, with a slight headache, and the sensation of a cold or a temperature on the way. Realising the late hour, and her missed morning's work, she dressed quickly and almost collided with her uncle on her way downstairs.

"Oops, never pass on the stairs!" he quipped – another of his late mother's superstitions which seemed to cover a multitude of minor daily events.

"Got to go, sorry," Cerys mumbled, sidling past him in her haste.

"Cerys, it's pouring out there!" Uncle Dom said, pausing mid-step, one hand on the bannister. (*"And you don't look well."* he refrained from saying out loud.) "Thursday's meant to be dry. Go to work then!"

"I said I'd be there; I can't just not show up." Cerys answered, searching frantically for her keys amongst the letters, teacups, loose change and other paraphernalia on the kitchen sideboard.

"Ces, there doesn't seem to be anyone there today anyway," Dom said quietly. "I wouldn't worry about going in this weather."

"What?!" Cerys stopped, halfway to the front door already. She felt a flash of ill-temper, out of character for her, and grappled with the ferocious sensation internally, as though it were a serpent about to strike. Her head thumped.

"How do you know that?"

"Well, I was out with Flowers earlier, and it started raining, and you were still in bed," Dom replied. "I thought I'd leave you to catch up on your beauty sleep, and since I was heading that way I'd call in to let your friend know that you'd be there another day. But I couldn't see any sign of Theresa or her grandmother."

Cerys drew a deep breath. Uncle Dom had gone to see Theresa, sought her out without Cerys's knowledge. Was that her uncle being helpful, or was it odd, and somewhat irksome – a thoughtful act, or an excuse to check up on both Theresa, and Cerys too?

" Maybe they went out somewhere?" Cerys shrugged her shoulders. She glanced out of the window at the dismal day – it was unlikely. Dom was right, it would be foolish to even think of gardening in that weather. The wind was picking up pace too, making the letterbox rattle, draughts echoing around upstairs in the way that they do in old houses.

"Ces, it looked like nobody's been there for decades – there's ivy growing over the doors?!" Dom, still mid-way up the stairs, looked down upon his niece's face and felt the difficult moment suspended between them like a tightrope, taught and dangerous, ready to snap, ready to spring back and hurl one or both of them off into the stratosphere, impossible to retrieve safely.

"What're you trying to say, Unc?" Cerys wanted to make light of the implication: it was a joke, surely - a forgettable tease. ""Cerys is cuckoo"?!" A little, gasping laugh escaped her and she turned to the hob, lifting the comfortingly garish, round kettle.

Dom was silent, unable to retract his observation, and afraid to antagonise the situation by saying more.

"I'm going to make some tea," Cerys said in a measured tone. "Hopefully we can re-start this whole conversation by the time the kettle's boiled. D'you want a cup?"

Dom sat down on a step, rubbing his hand over his face. The icy moment was broken and he said, " Of course. Let's start the day again hey." And then, suddenly, inexplicably:

"I'd really love it if you'd come to the church with me one Sunday."

"Huh?!" Cerys exclaimed, turning back to face him, her eyebrows raised in surprise. "Where did that come from?!"

Dom could not answer that question; it was not a premeditated request and had come straight from his heart before he had time to consider. But as soon as the words had escaped him he felt wholly that it had been the right thing to say, in spite of his niece's expression of shock and amusement. Weighted silence returned between them.

Cerys, still reeling from the dangerous conversation that had just been evaded neatly thought *"Oh my God, he's serious!"*

"Aw, come on Unc…you know that's not really my thing." She shook her tired head softly, willing the kettle to hurry up and boil.

"I don't see how turning up to a weekly lecture by someone who doesn't even know me can solve anyone's problems."

"It's not just about the service though, Cerys, or the "lecture."" Dom spread his hands, struggling to find the right words. "It's the act of drawing closer to God, of building a structure there, you know? Having a solid foundation to stand upon, when life gets difficult "

Cerys suddenly slapped the teaspoon she was holding down upon the sideboard, and whirled around to face Dom. The tightrope was frayed to it's last strands now. Exhaustion and fear from the last sleepless night overwhelmed her, and Dom's unintentionally hurtful suggestion, that she had somehow imagined a strange woman had convinced her to begin working at an uninhabited property, still burned fiercely in her mind.

"Well going to church didn't help Nanny Grieg, did it?! God didn't help her when she was laying on the kitchen floor, alone and dying in her flat, did he?! *HE* didn't help her, and nor did we! I was asleep in a bed on the floor above her, and I didn't hear her, or help her! *Where was God then?!"*

Cerys was shaking now, and great, undignified sobs wrenched themselves noisily from the pit of her stomach. Her head, shoulders and arms convulsed with their force. It was as if someone had pulled the plug on her soul and all Cerys's grief and sorrow that had built up after Nanny Grieg's death flooded out from her unchecked.

Dom, frozen to the spot during her furious outburst, broke his position at the sight of her breakdown and came down the stairs two at a time. He hugged her hard, his chin pressed in to the top of her skull, his long arms squeezing Cerys's own to her sides as she shook where she stood.

"Hey,hey,hey,hey,hey," Dom found himself repeating quietly, over and over, until the sobs and shaking stilled and Cerys stood limply, her face pressed messily into her uncle's sweatshirt, almost afraid to pull it away. At that moment, it felt like the only thing holding her up was her uncle, and if either of them moved she might just crumple into a damp-faced heap on the kitchen floor.

"I'll make the bloody tea," Dom said eventually. They both stifled a ridiculous laugh, borne out of the hysteria. Cerys covered her mouth with her hands, wide-eyed. How could she even think of laughter now, after throwing this terrible, awkward verbal bomb into their crowd of two?

"You go back to bed, Ces," Dom continued, retrieving the teaspoon from where it had bounced violently off the kitchen side and under the table. "I'll leave it outside your door."

Cerys stared at the floor stricken with shame.

"I'm sorry, Unc," she said. "I'm sorry for being...mean. I know you were trying to help."

"Don't worry about it, Ces," Dom said, waving the apology aside. "Really. Maybe it was the wrong moment to try and be a missionary." He shrugged, self-deprecatingly, suddenly feeling clumsy and foolish. Cerys had a fleeting mental image of her uncle dressed in khaki and carrying a musket, preaching the Bible to indigenous tribes in some distant, hot jungle, picking the snakes out of his boots at night. It made her smile. She turned towards the stairs.

"It wasn't your fault, by the way," Dom called after her. "About your nan. It was a shitty way to go. But any number of things could have happened - or not. She could have got cancer and suffered a long miserable death. She could have been gone already before she hit the floor, and never knew what was happening. That's what I pray for. But you weren't to blame, Cerys, for any of it."

"'K," Cerys nodded, her gaze on her feet still. She was unconvinced but too drained to enter into any more emotional discussion. She knew that the only way to put events in to any kind of perspective was to get some sleep, and she returned to her un-made bed and surrendered at last to it, lulled by the sound of steady, grey rain.

*

Cerys awoke in the early evening, feeling refreshed, and, her uncle noticed with some relief, looking much healthier. She was also very hungry. They bought fish and chips from the van outside the pub: the smell of salt and vinegar and chips frying fresh were too good to resist. Easy conversation was reinstated between them by the sharing of the slightly guilty pleasure of junky, comfort food.

Uncle Dom had to be away early the next morning, he told Cerys- a live audience capture for a breakfast show, starting work at a hideous hour. Cerys lay in bed later that night, her sleeping pattern muddled, conscious of not disturbing her uncle ahead of his three a.m. alarm call. Her thoughts were busy in the quiet room.

She would go to Theresa's, she resolved, in the morning, if there was a break in the weather. She considered the evidence of Theresa's existence - the fraught conversation with her uncle troubled her deeply now that she had had a chance to think over his words.

The notes Theresa had paid Cerys with for the gardening work were not exactly sound evidence. Cerys dismissed the idea of presenting the little brown bottle that Theresa had bestowed her to her uncle - he and her mother would likely have a fit if they knew about that.

Cerys wondered if she could show him the amulet as proof at least of a gift from Theresa, but realised that sort of thing might be found in any flea market or second- hand

61

shop. The amulet was no reliable confirmation of Cerys's interaction with either of the Volk women.

Cerys unwound the thing from around her neck – it was surprisingly weighty – she was regretfully aware that she was more comfortable without it. Instead she kept it scrunched up in her hand, as a compromise: a talisman against the night.

The familiar hateful dark energy crept in to the room with the passing of slow hours, and peppered the air like a plague of black flies, buzzing around Cerys's head, irritating and irrational, depriving her of her peace.

She ignored the sensations for as long as she could and then succumbed to switching on the soft bedside lamp and watching the shadows playing on the curtains as infrequent cars passed in the street below.

It was with relief that she heard her uncle stirring finally in the early hours, preparing to leave for work, treading softly about the house as he organised himself for the day ahead.

She ventured downstairs and answered his question, "Bad night?" with a sheepish shrug.

"Sorry I can't stop," Dom glanced up at the kitchen clock. "You going to be ok?"

"'Course," Cerys nodded, not wanting to delay him. "I'll be fine."

"And don't forget Mrs Devin's being brought home today." Dom reminded her. "When you go in to see old Flowers. She might be upstairs in bed or something. Let her know you're in the house or she might get a scare. We don't want her back in hospital again!"

"Of course," said Cerys, lifting the latch and opening the door for her uncle to wheel his case through. A flood of silver dawn-light and fresh, damp air breezed in, vital and sweet. Cerys felt the troubling cloud surrounding her dispel instantly with the chorus of the birds and the hum of Uncle Dom's car engine warming up somewhere around the corner.

She was able to fall into a deep, comforting sleep then, for a few hours. Although it was not for very long, it was enough to enable Cerys to be up and dressed and feeling reasonable before ten a.m. She could have slept for a lot longer but she did not know what time Mrs Devin would be returned. She hated to think of patient Flowers, alone and waiting anxiously for someone to come. Cerys used the spare key to let herself in to Mrs Devin's house and paused uncertainly in the quiet gloom.

"'Lo?" A disembodied voice floated through from the rear of the house.

"Mrs Devin?" Cerys followed the call to the doorway of a small dining room that led off the kitchen and faced out onto the narrow back garden. "It's Cerys, Dominic's niece. Is it ok to come in?"

"Yes, yes, c'min 'ere, Cerys, do," the fragile voice answered from within the cramped room. "They've put me in 'ere 'til I'm steady on my feet again. So I won't havta do the stairs, you see."

Cerys saw that Mrs Devin was laid in a large bed on wheels, the kind that tilts and raises and lowers at each end at the press of a button. It had a whirring hospital mattress plugged in at the wall, intended to prevent bed sores. Cerys recognised the steady hum from visits to the hospital where her mum worked as she approached Mrs Devin's side.

"Thankyou so much for lookin' after my little boy," Mrs Devin croaked, reaching out a dry hand towards Cerys's arm. Cerys was reminded of a bird's clawed foot, curled and brittle, and resisted the urge to pull away from her touch. Nanny Grieg's hands had always been warm and smooth and nimble-fingered despite her age.

63

"Ah, it's no problem at all," she said, aware suddenly of the dog nestled at her feet under the bed. "He's a good boy, aren't you Flowers? How are *you* feeling, Mrs Devin?"

Mrs Devin see-sawed one of her curled hands, which were mapped with raised veins of a violent purple, and red, swollen knuckles, indicating "so-so." Her crinkled cheeks still dimpled as she smiled up at Cerys. "Well, you don't exackly 'spect to feel marvellous at my age, you know." And then, casually, " You bin workin ' up at that 'ouse, I hear?"

"I have." Cerys replied cautiously, wondering what Mrs Devin had heard, if anything. Perhaps she was simply trying to draw gossip from Cerys about Theresa and her grandmother and the condition of their house in it's fascinating state of neglect? Any information would be thoroughly speculated over amongst the villagers, Cerys was sure. She had no desire to be part of it, so she did not elaborate.

" All us old ones remember that place," Mrs Devin nodded gravely. " We was all scared of it, growin' up 'ere in the village, like."

"Why?" Cerys's own curiosity was piqued. Her own encounters with the house had not left her afraid. If anything, her sympathy had grown towards the sad-looking property, and the garden that she felt ought to be loved and looked after, and could be made really quite beautiful.

"'T'was empty, far's we knew, since our own mothers and fathers was tiny children." Mrs Devin continued, her reflective mood warming. "But there was always some talk of an 'ole lady bein' seen upstairs at the window. That story got bandied about every now and then. We used to run up to the front door for dares, like, when we was playin' out as kids. Screeching like banshees no doubt. No wonder the 'ole lady was said to 'ave a look on her like murder!"

Cerys stood very still, her breath slowed right down tight in her chest, her heart beating achingly loud in her own ears as she listened to Mrs Devin's increasingly animated voice.

"We was all told not to go near though, mind!" she wagged a hooked index finger at Cerys. "My gran' mother used to say "Rum things go in that 'ouse, Liza! You steer clear o' them women. They'se outside the law, that family."

"How do you mean?" Cerys asked quietly, biting her lip to still her ragged nerves.

"Well now," Mrs Devin continued. "She said that way back when *she* were a nipper, village folk used to go there if they 'ad a problem to fix, like. Mostly the womenfolk. But…there was always a price. "Nothin' gets done for free," thass what my gran would say."

Cerys crouched down by Flowers' bed, stroking his velvet ears gently, her gaze fixed on the floor as she tried to appear only casually interested in Mrs Devin's recollections. All the while, her heart was thumping a steady drumbeat and a high-pitched tone seared in her head as she quietly waited for the old lady to go on.

"How do you mean – *problems*?" Cerys asked from her hunched position. She was eye-level with the metal bars on the hospital bed, speaking through them as though she were a prisoner at Mrs Devin's side.

Mrs Devin raised a hairy eyebrow, considering Cerys's capacity as teenage confidante, and evidently judged her capable of handling such ancient and weighty village lore, for she answered in measured tone:

" A drunk for an 'usband. Maybe one who liked to use 'is fists at 'ome. A poor harvest. Baby on the way and another four mouths to feed. A lan'lord takin' more than a sheaf of corn and the rent from the tenant farmers wife, if you get me. A birthmark. A hare-lip. All manner o' things

65

what made life 'streamly difficult for wimmin in them days."

Mrs Devin craned her weathered face off the pillow and over towards Cerys, peering tortoise-like through the bars.

"You mind yourself over there, girl!" she nodded at Cerys, frowning deeply. "They was known to 'elp Quaintlip people...and there was those that come from a long way to buy their...*services,* shall we say. But my gran always said that there was ... what was the word she used? Ca – Vee – Atts. That was it. *Caveats.* She said there was a darkness in that big old 'ouse and sometimes folk got more than they'd bargained for."

Cerys suddenly felt that she very much wanted to be outdoors again. The air had become close and stuffy in the makeshift bedroom, condensed with the weight of Mrs Devin's words and the intensity with which she had imparted her story. Cerys stood up, pins and needles sparking in her legs, and shook Flowers' lead loose at her side.

"Sounds like interesting stuff, Mrs Devin," Cerys said cheerily. "I bet Flowers is keen to go out by now though." And without waiting for a response from his owner, she said "C'mon then, Mister," and roused him from the comfort of his basket. "You must be bursting at the seams. We'll be back shortly, Mrs Devin, OK? I'll make you some tea before I go."

"You mind yourself, " Mrs Devin repeated solemnly, her eyes still fixed on Cerys's face, which hovered like a pale moon now above her in the half-light. "A young girl like you. I dunno who's back living in that big 'ouse now but it's bound to be one o' them tricky wimmin. Tricky, tricky, tricky..." Her voice tailed off drowsily, head resting back on the pillow again as she succumbed to medicated fatigue.

The light outside was luminous, dreamy from the rain, the birds singing their hearts out and criss-crossing from rooftop to lamp post and swooping dangerously close to the tops of passing cars. Cerys pulled up the soft hood of her jacket, shielding her eyes which were now sensitive even to these pearly, muted daylight tones. She and Flowers walked without direction, ambling through the cobbled side-streets and cut-through alleys of the village. They passed a sequence of old cottages and Cerys noted their names with childish pleasure - "The Coffin-Makers'" and "Candle Corner" being her favourites , she decided.

Cerys wondered if Theresa and her grandmother's house had a name, and what it might be if so. Her mind was in some considerable turmoil after her encounter with Mrs Devin. Cerys could no longer dismiss her growing disquiet regarding the place- and indeed about Theresa- as the result of her own over-active imagination. She *had* seen that face at the window in the night, and she was apparently not the only person ever to have experienced that furious, ghastly glare. Whatever was happening to her since arriving in Quaintlip was beyond Cerys's usual remit of understanding. She was no longer sure she wanted to return to the house, to lose hours to working in the garden, or even to see Theresa again soon. She would put off the gardening there for another day or two, she decided, and spend some proper time working in Uncle Dom's garden instead. She had done virtually nothing there so far, and he was family. Surely he deserved her appreciation more than a strange new friend whom Cerys had only just met?

Cerys avoided walking past Theresa's house and that end of the village altogether, consciously trying to put some distance between herself and the place. She eventually found herself at the top of the steep track which lead to the church, where the creamy white hawthorn blossom was

67

now sodden and dripping from the trees after the heavy rain, and blackbirds sang overhead from spiny branches.

She and Flowers strolled under the arch of the lych-gate and followed the towering curves of the main stone church building all the way around its circumference. Cerys, lost in her thoughts, trailed a hand loosely across the flint as she went, drawing a circle around the building, as though she were trying to claim some of it's peace for her own troubled mind.

There was something comforting, Cerys felt, in being in such close proximity to that immense structure, which had held up strong and steadfast over the centuries, much longer than any of the countless lives which had passed through it, cradle to grave, and lived alongside of it in the village below.

As Cerys rounded the North wall for a second time, she raised her eyes from the wet grass and with unhappy surprise saw Theresa, seated on a small wooden bench, staring, unblinking, at Cerys as if she had been waiting there for her for some time.

Cerys froze, a rabbit caught in headlights.

"Mornin'" Theresa greeted her, her face blank, un-smiling. "Where you bin' hiding?"

(*"As if she read my mind!"*) thought Cerys, guiltily.

"Hi," she replied levelly. "I've been under the weather. I don't have your number or I would have called you yesterday to let you know I wasn't coming over. Sorry."

"I don't have a phone." Theresa shrugged. "You bin' sleeping much, have you?"

Cerys's heart told her that she did not feel like sharing at that moment. She had too much to process in her mind, on far too little sleep. Her unreasonable outburst at Uncle Dom yesterday, the enormity of the blame that Cerys felt with regards to her grandmother's death, all the strange events after bonding with Theresa and then Mrs Devin's sinister recollections about Theresa's house and family…Under other circumstances Cerys would probably have construed these as no more than the spooky village gossip of older and superstitious generations, but the mention of the same terrifying face at the window -that Cerys herself had seen- had shaken her. She answered Theresa briefly, hoping that she did not sound as jittery as she felt.

"Not great, but I'll manage. I'll be back to work in a couple of days. Just need to catch up a bit. I'll see you then." Cerys tugged on Flowers' lead and walked softly past the bench where Theresa remained seated, studying Cerys's face intently, her long dark hair clamped to her temples by the now-drizzling rain.

"You didn't try my medicine, then." Theresa stated, as Cerys passed her by. Her coal-black eyes were fixed on Cerys's face: Cerys could feel them actively bearing into her as she resisted meeting Theresa's gaze.

"Maybe try it tonight," Cerys nodded. "Have a good day, Theresa. I'll see you soon."

It took all of Cerys's strength to keep her composure and not break into a run as she kept walking steadily away from Theresa, still sat upon the bench in sullen silence like a crow guarding carrion. She could sense Theresa's eyes fixed on her and dared not look back. Once she reached the other side of the church she let out a long breath of tension and lengthened her strides down the hill and back out on to the road once more.

Cerys focused her eyes straight ahead, afraid that if she glanced left or right she would catch sight of Theresa again - maybe standing in the shadows under the yew trees or waiting at the stile at the bottom of the footpath. She did not feel strong enough to cross her path again so soon. She knew it was irrational – what on earth did she think Theresa would do to her? All Cerys knew was that she had almost

69

certainly offended her, and that Theresa was definitely angry.

When she reached the high street, Cerys scooped up Flowers, who was lagging behind in a disgruntled manner, his short legs unaccustomed to such haste. Cerys held him close as she half-walked, half-jogged back to Mrs Devin's house, the little dog's smooth body reassuringly solid and warm in her arms.

She knocked politely at Mrs Devin's door, just in case someone else might be visiting, or the carers early for their tea time call. Letting herself in to the house, Cerys followed Flowers as he padded through to the small back room. She considered finding her way around the kitchen in order to make Mrs Devin a cup of tea.

Cerys felt an odd prickle around her temples and on the nape of her neck upon stepping over the threshold to the dining room. Everything was just a she had left it : the ancient refrigerator whirring in the kitchen, the Bakelite clock ticking on the mantlepiece in the front room. China dogs winked from a useless shelf in the dim hallway. But a silence laid heavily upon the rooms in spite of the familiar everyday sounds and the ornaments which had decorated the passing decades.

Cerys knew before she reached Mrs Devin's bedside that she was dead. The sight of her face, drained of colour, and eyes fixed glassily upon the ceiling only confirmed what Cerys already sensed in her spirit. For a long moment, it felt to Cerys that she and the old lady were captured briefly in a quiet, still orb together, perfectly un-noticed by the universe which marched on regardless, as is it's natural order. Then shock broke through the glassy walls of that orb, and Cerys turned and fled next door, leaving the bewildered dog in his basket and the front door wide open.

Part Three

The funeral was arranged for the following Friday. Having recalled the details of when she last spoke with Mrs Devin, and how she had found her very-recently-deceased body, to the ambulance crew, to her uncle, to Mrs Devin's daughter Elaine (over the telephone – she had been due to come up from London for Quaintlip that very evening) and to her own mother (also over the telephone, in London) Cerys was not keen to repeat the sorry story multiple times to Quaintlip residents. She was pretty sure that she would be stopped in the street, the little shop, or wherever she walked Flowers, by well-meaning but curious folk. She understood that this sort of news was the life-blood of a community such as this and would be bread-and- butter as far as neighbourly conversation was concerned for at least a month. But Cerys felt no satisfaction or personal ownership in being the bearer of the sad details. She was not family or a close friend, and had no connection with Mrs Devin apart from neighbourliness by default. She would leave it to Elaine to share the story if she chose.

So Cerys spent the next few days indoors, in her room at Uncle Dom's, watching films on her laptop, and reading. Her uncle tactfully left her in peace. Cerys slept poorly, awake for hours at a time during the night, rising at mid-day lethargic, and low in spirits. On Saturday, Dom suggested a trip into town, mainly with a view to browsing the various second-hand bookshops. ("And to get you out into some daylight," his concern for his niece voiced itself silently.)

They spent a pleasant afternoon side-stepping the crowds in the market square, who were queuing and jostling for fruit and veg and fresh seafood from the stalls. The heavenly scent of bread and pastries filled the air , along with the clamour of voices and stallholders hawking their goods at a high volume. Dom and Cerys wove in and out of book stalls and charity shops, window-shopping and gazing

71

up at the architecture of the Tudor buildings around them. Dark beams and sagging rooftops held up impossibly-lofty structures, and intriguingly ugly gargoyles guarded the doorways to the ancient church which stood centrally in the market square.

They decided to finish their outing by stopping for coffee and cake, and sat at a tiny metal table outside a small café just off the high street. Cerys almost began to feel better for being away from Quaintlip for the day, for being anonymous and part of the crowd.

While her uncle queued inside, Cerys leafed through a local newspaper which had been left on their table. She found herself remarkably unsurprised to read a short report – only a couple of paragraphs – about a body found in woodland on the county borders. "Michael Buck, 61, was well-known to county police, for indecent exposure and other sexual offences. Police had not been able to gather enough evidence with which to convict him and his victims had been unwilling to attend court. Coroners confirmed a heart attack as cause of death. He lived alone, and leaves no next-of-kin."

There was a grainy photo of a younger Michael Buck, still recognisable to Cerys as the man who had approached she and Theresa in the graveyard some weeks ago. With a numbness in her heart, and the odd sensation of a sort of grey screen drawing shut in her mind, she folded the newspaper back over and pushed it calmly away from her, as her uncle reappeared to join her at the table.

The grey screen remained in place as Uncle Dom and Cerys shared their coffees, skimmed through books they had chosen, and people-watched for a while. It enveloped Cerys's thoughts and all her emotional responses to the events and discoveries of the past few days, keeping them neatly bound just at the edge of consciousness, while she gazed flatly out at the busy street and absorbed the continuous cacophony of voices, traffic, coffee machines hissing and spluttering, crates clattering to the cobbles as the traders began to pack up the stalls, and the clock on the church tower chimed deafeningly, four times, resonating eerily throughout the crowds and echoing off the old buildings surrounding it.

Cerys wondered at first if she ought to be worried, by the sudden shut-down of all feeling she was experiencing. It was as though she were viewing the world from behind glass, or watching it on television. It didn't belong to her and she didn't belong to it. After a while, she relaxed into the odd state of mind. Some part of her understood that her own brain was trying to protect her from all the things she could not process safely yet. It was actually quite a relief to just stop *feeling* for once.

Later that evening, Cerys was also not surprised to hear a loud knock at the front door – one which her uncle apparently did not hear. Perhaps he had his headphones on, Cerys thought. He was trying to arrange his work schedule on the dated computer in his small study. Cerys knew without having to look that it was Theresa knocking. She waited a few moments then peered furtively through a slight gap in her bedroom curtains, trying her hardest not to stir them; holding her breath. *Grey screen- breathe in. One, two, three, four...Don't move. Grey screen- breathe out.* She watched the hunched figure of Theresa eventually stomp away purposefully, head down, hands in pockets, not looking back. Cerys had no doubt that Theresa knew she was home. She would face her, when she was ready. She just wanted to stay in this emotionless grey pocket for a little while longer.

Later that night, the tapping began at Cerys's bedroom window. Softly at first, then, just when Cerys started to drift into sleep it became loud and insistent, making her heart pound. She did not dare to peep out of the curtains this time

73

. Her bedroom was ten feet up off the ground. Whatever the cause of the rapping on the glass - the deranged demand for her attention – it was inhuman and it felt *bad,* and Cerys had no wish to see it. She buried her head under the duvet and lay, paralysed with suppressed fear, until dawn.

The next morning, Cerys got up late again to find the house empty. It was Sunday and Uncle Dom had gone to church. He had left a note by the kettle.

"Come for coffee at the hall if you like. 12p.m."

Cerys's stomach knotted up even at the thought of attending a church service and feeling all those curious eyes upon her. She had no idea of the protocol for a non-believer. She was pretty certain that she would stand up at the wrong time or utter a resounding " Amen" outside of the congregation's collective voice, leaving her to feel foolish and exposed as a fraud. However, at this strange juncture in her life, the idea of meeting her uncle in the parish hall and being safely absorbed amongst a group of generally well-meaning folk appealed to her. She was sure that there would be no sinister knocks or tapping noises tormenting her whilst in the company of the church crowd. There would be no weighted, dark atmosphere hanging over her there.

Cerys also felt that it would be courteous to meet her uncle halfway with his suggestion that she join him at church. After her previous horrendous outburst in response to his offer, she still wished with all her heart to make amends in some way. Cerys realised that she would encounter many questions from the villagers about her discovery of Mrs Devin. But perhaps, she reasoned, it would be better to embrace it all in one sweep, and get it out of the way. She could not hide indoors all Summer, especially not with the frightening things that were happening to her. She would go. It would be a good thing to do, she told herself firmly.

Cerys pulled on clean jeans, white-ish trainers and a favourite cobalt-blue t-shirt with a bright white star front-centre. She wound her long, pale-copper hair up on the top of her head, drawing her straight fringe smoothly down with a fine comb. She pocketed her keys, and paused to caress Flower's crinkled velvet head. His brown eyes questioned her movements from his position, curled up on the small sofa in the front room. Uncle Dom had relented to Cerys's pleas that Flowers should not be placed in kennels or given to a shelter. The dog had rapidly been absorbed seamlessly into their daily lives.

"Be back soon, Pup." Cerys promised him, and she took a deep breath, straightened up and slipped out of the house.

Cerys found her uncle in conversation with a woman of perhaps fifty. They were standing together outside of the parish hall, which was set back a little from the road, at the bottom of the steep hill which led to the church. Evidently, the gathering of church-goers had decided to move outdoors after the service, and enjoy the late May weather. The air was indeed as sweet and warm as vanilla, and the intensity of the greens and shadows in the depths of the horse chestnut trees and the tall grass were as dramatic and rousing as thunder. It would have been unforgivable to stay indoors on a day like this, Cerys thought. She sidled in shyly next to Dom, and squeezed his arm gently in silent greeting, not wishing to interrupt.

"Ah, Cerys, you're here!"

Cerys felt a glow in her heart at the expression of pleased surprise in her uncle's voice.

"This is my niece!" Dom introduced her to the woman he had been talking with. She wore a very long, vivid blue summer dress, the colour of which exactly mirrored Cerys's t-shirt.

"So glad to meet you at last!" The woman greeted Cerys with a generous, open smile, and nodded towards Cerys's top.

"We are matching, I see!" she added happily. Cerys warmed to her instantly, the tight knot in her stomach dissolving like sugar in water.

"This is Margaret," Uncle Dom gestured to his acquaintance. "Tea? Coffee, either of you?"

"I'd love a tea, please," Cerys answered, glad to have something to hold, to center herself amongst the small crowd. Elderly ladies bustled in to where she and Margaret stood, making pleasant small talk, itching to strike up conversation with quite possibly the only seventeen-year-old in Quaintlip at that moment in time, and especially one with a relatively dramatic story regarding Mrs Devin, who had been one of their own church family there.

"D'you want to go and sit down over there, Cerys? Under that big tree?" Margaret asked cheerily. "I've been here since half-eight this morning with the Toddlers at the Cross group, and I've not been home since. I'm fit to collapse. More like Cross Toddlers this morning, it was. They all got out of bed the wrong side today!"

With Uncle Dom now talking with another lady, having dispatched two mugs of tea their way, Cerys was grateful for Margaret's suggestion, which she understood to be her way of removing Cerys from the friendly interrogation, however well-intentioned it was.

She followed Margaret over to a vast fallen bough , which appeared to have lain a long time beneath an ivy-stricken old oak. The tree's spreading branches made concentric shadows on the soft grass before them, a crazed Celtic knot contrasting dark and light on a tousled carpet of green. Cerys was reminded of the aged, twisted oak in Theresa's garden, and the back of her neck prickled with the mental association, the tension inside her returning.

Cerys and Margaret sat in comfortable silence for a few moments, people-watching, breathing in the day. Cerys fought internally against thoughts of Theresa and her house, her garden, her sullen furious glare, and the night of despairing fear and solitude to come. It couldn't last forever, this...*thing*. Surely? Then, unprompted, Margaret said calmly:

"You have a dreadful spirit of fear attached to you, Cerys."

"I'm sorry?!" Cerys stared at Margaret, sat next to her on the bough with her hands in the lap of her gloriously vivid dress, cradling her tea.

"I don't mean to freak you out. I'm sorry if I have." Margaret continued. She was gazing at a group of children a little distance away who were attempting noisily to organise a rounders game between them all. Margaret spoke as matter-of-factly as though she had just observed a slight change in the weather, Cerys thought with alarm.

"I can sense the spirits linked to people quite often," she continued. "I've been doing it since I was twenty, or thereabouts. It's a gift, a spiritual gift. Sometimes it can feel like a curse. But it's not intended to frighten anyone."

Cerys was silent, uncertain how to respond, instinctively defensive but conscious that this woman - crazy or not – was a friend of her uncle and she had to remain courteous.

"I have no idea what you're talking about, sorry." Cerys said eventually, with a little laugh. "I'm pretty sure it's got nothing to do with me, though. I just came here for a cup of tea with my uncle!"

Margaret faced Cerys, smiling, her clear blue eyes warm and serious.

"I'm not talking about spirits as in *ghosts* or something silly like that, Cerys! Have you ever read about or heard of discernment, or demonic attacks, or spiritual affliction? Anything like that at all?"

"No. No I haven't." Cerys answered somewhat sullenly, facing away from Margaret again and pretending to be interested in the messy rounders game being launched.

Unfazed, Margaret sat forward, and placed her cup in the grass where it sat drunkenly, cooling tea lurching towards the rim. She put a hand lightly on Cerys's forearm, and said "Well, I can sense the fear surrounding you…attached to you… it's like being in a python's grip, isn't it? Please let me help you. Let God help you. It's not easy but you *can* break free of it, you really can!"

All of a sudden, Cerys felt, horrifyingly, that she wanted very much to cry, although she couldn't imagine a less appropriate moment to do so. Then anger flashed through her like lightning and she stood up, stiffly.

"I don't know what a discerner of spirits is, or any of that stuff, and I don't *want* to, thankyou. I've been up to my neck in weird…*shit* since I arrived here, and I don't need any more! " Cerys was shocked at her own lack of composure. Her own voice sounded nasal and whiny, and her throat felt choked with sobs fighting to escape her.

"Thanks for your concern!"

("Hold it together, for fuck's sake, Cerys.") she berated herself silently, standing up, the small spell of reverie broken now. And she walked away, head down, waving briefly at her uncle as she wove her way hastily through the gathering.

*

"Cerys, you up there?" Uncle Dom called out on his return to the house later that afternoon. Cerys, curled up on her bed, groaned inwardly at the sound of his cheerful voice. She screwed her eyes shut tight and put both hands

78

over her head; a weak attempt at un-hearing her uncle. His booted feet clattered lightly up the stairs and Cerys sensed him pause outside her door.

"Margaret asked me to pass on her number to you. Did you get the chance to chat much?"

"She said to call her any time," he eventually continued, the silence from within willing him away. *"Perhaps she's sleeping,"* he reasoned, dismayed somewhat. He had been convinced that Margaret, of all the people he knew, would be the one who could reach Cerys, if that was the right term. It would be a far healthier sisterly bond than the one Cerys seemed to cherished with the unsavoury Theresa. Instinct told him that Cerys was not asleep and did not wish to talk.

"I'll do lunch, ok?" Dom stooped and slid the contact card under Cerys's bedroom door. Relenting, guiltily, Cerys tried to sound as bright and normal as she was able.

"Sorry, earphones in! Be down in a minute!"

She waited until Dom had gone back downstairs, and she heard assorted metallic thuds as he drew pans out of the kitchen cupboards and lit the oven. She slid off the bed then, and on hands and knees crept over to where the little card lay on the smooth floorboards. Printed in neat capitals were the name "Margaret Russell. Parish Council of St Mary and St Botolph." A mobile and landline number were given.

Cerys sat cross-legged, on the floor, for a few moments and picked the card up. She weighed it on her upturned palm like a precious jewel. She was so tired she could not even think what to *think* about Margaret Russell, and what she had said at the church, and its implications for Cerys. She wearily pocketed the card, and leant her forehead against the cool wood of the door. She had *liked* Margaret, really warmed to her. But she had liked Theresa, too. Cerys wondered briefly if the unlikeable woman here was herself

– impulsive and trusting, yet too quick to withdraw her friendship when things weren't quite as she had expected?

The first tiny knocks came at the window then, subtle and measured, like distant Morse code.

"*Fuck,fuck,fuck,no!* "she cursed through gritted teeth. "Not in daylight too, you have *got* to be kidding me." She hunched forward, grinding her knuckles with painful force into her ears.

Tap, tap, tap. Tap, tap.. pause.

Tap, tap, tap.

Cerys clenched her jaw, willing herself not to cry out. She forced herself to stand, without looking back at the closed window pane, and went downstairs with determination, to fuss Flowers and to offer a hand with peeling vegetables in the oven-warmed kitchen.

*

With Monday looming, and her uncle due to be working until late in the evening, Cerys made a conscious decision to concentrate on his garden. She desperately needed distraction and something tangible and positive to focus on. She had no desire now to return to the house at the end of the village, and she fervently hoped that Theresa would not seek her out at Uncle Dom's place again. Hopefully, she and her grandmother would find someone else to deal with their garden before too long. A couple of lads, thick-skinned and oblivious to the occasional peculiar customer, with their own truck and machinery, would be far better suited to the job, Cerys reasoned. They would finish the job in half the time it would take Cerys by herself.

Cerys acknowledged – at least to herself that her sleepless nights were not improving since coming to Quaintlip. If anything, since her association with Theresa and her house, they had become a great deal worse. She missed her mum and had seriously considered going back to London – there would be no Theresa lurking in the shadows and turning up unannounced there. But Cerys would feel terribly guilty if she went home early - she knew Uncle Dom would be worried, and she didn't want him to feel as though he had failed her somehow.

She had placed the amulet that Theresa had given her under her bed, along with the little bottle of brown liquid. The feel of the leathery ribbon against her own skin repelled her, and she did not want the temptation of seeing the sunlight glint warmly in the amber glass, inviting her to try just one sip, because it might just help her sleep, it might just make everything better... and what then? Cerys supposed she would have to maintain the relationship with Theresa falsely in order to gain more of the "remedy" when it ran out, if it really worked. She had neither the will or the energy to enter into that kind of game-playing with a woman who, quite frankly, frightened Cerys to some extent now.

Dom left at nine, seeming distracted. When Cerys asked whether he was alright he shrugged and grinned.

"Monday Blues, I expect," he said, shaking his head as if to rid himself of an irritating fly. Or a full moon, or something. Nothing a decent coffee won't fix!" It was out of character for him. Cerys wondered just how much her being there, and being *her,* was affecting him.

Once he was gone, Cerys gathered herself together and drove to a plant nursery, which was a distance enough away for her to feel a slight sense of unburdening as the fields rolled away and miles passed between her and the village.

She relaxed amongst the aisles of shrubs and plants at the nursery: here, she was on solid ground, surrounded by the familiar names and colours and textures of leaf and petal and pollen. Rich cherry-coloured roses and their heavenly perfume contrasted with the heady tang of marigolds, rust and brandy-coloured, crowded in trays on wooden pallets. Tiny, coral-like alpines and succulents curled and spiked

81

over the edges of pots filled with light loose grit, like alien creatures, or jewels from the sea bed. Awful canned music played overhead, tinny and tacky, reminding Cerys of the busier world outside of Quaintlip's charming but subdued rurality. She was amongst people here, ignorant of trouble such as hers' and she felt she could breathe easy for a short time.

Thinking past the summer months, Cerys chose white vinca and hellebores, conscious of the shady flint walls in the enclosed garden. Both would be a surprise for Dom when they began to bloom in late winter. She also picked out bedding plants, to brighten the pots now - trailing pelargoniums in salmon pink and white, and indigo and honey-coloured violas with tiny, nodding lion faces. A familiar flame of excitement and enthusiasm were building within her; she loved to start a new garden project, however small and humble. She would hold the idea like a torch in her mind's eye, until her plans materialised, and then, when it was finished, she would be able to lay the shining image down to rest with peaceful satisfaction.

She returned to the village, shoving her car confidently up on the pavement outside her uncle's house in order to unload. *"And to hell with the neighbours this time!"* she thought. They could watch her park badly and drop things as she went back and forth into the house if they wanted to - she found she no longer cared.

She began by clearing the courtyard, ready to begin. It was a warm, mellow day, and Cerys dosed herself generously with coffee and biscuits as she swept last year's crisped leaves from the cobbles and emptied spent soil from the neglected pots standing on the gravel. She managed to salvage a deep purple clematis, choked by bindweed against the far wall. Cerys freed it up from its prison and tied it carefully so that it could reach the sun.

She hooked out yellowing grass from between the cobbles, and scraped away oozing handfuls of spongy, dark moss. In doing so, Cerys delighted in discovering that there were patterns in the cobbles, in different shades of stone – circles and loops of butterscotch and sandy hues interspersed with sea greys and lavender tones. Her hair swept the cobbles as she scrubbed and scraped, hunched over them. She had to keep swiping her fringe out of her eyes; her face had grown sticky with heat.

Finally, Cerys hauled a slightly battered metal bird bath from its place of abandonment buried in wasp-ridden ivy. She scrubbed it and set it on its clawed feet, and filled it with tap water. "Not bad!" she smiled at it: a sweet and fitting centre-piece for the little garden. Perhaps the small birds would visit this place now and bring her uncle some pleasure watching them drink and bathe, long after she had gone back to London.

Cerys felt something close to a sense of well-being as she worked, better than she had felt for weeks. Her fatigue was a healthy one this afternoon, borne of the enthusiastic physical work outdoors. She tidied her tools away, gave one last sweep-round with the dustpan and brush, watered the new plants in thoroughly and finally removed her gloves and trainers before stepping in to the comparatively dark house. Uncle Dom was due home around eight that evening; she looked forward to surprising him with the newly-transformed garden.

As Cerys entered the kitchen, her eyes still adjusting from bright sunlight to the cool, dark shades indoors, a tall, stretched figure silhouetted against the front door spoke her name. With a sickening jolt of horror, Cerys realised that it Theresa stood there, with her back to the front door and her hands spread against it like claws, as if she were holding it tightly shut against the world.

"Theresa!" Cerys faltered. "What are you doing…in here?"

"Front door was unlocked," Theresa answered unapologetically. "I came to check on you. You never come back to finish the garden."

The blind in the kitchen was drawn down to keep the sun out and the old house cool: Theresa's eyes were black holes in the gloom, glittering with amusement or rage, Cerys could not tell. She suspected the latter: Theresa's Cheshire-cat cat smile was not forthcoming this time. She immediately sensed the brittle chill of her night-terrors descend upon the room. The familiar, bristling static in the air, almost audible, made her skin crawl. Cerys realised with heavy dismay that the hideous sensation was not confined to the night time any more. It could manifest at any hour, and had never been so strong as it was at this moment. Cerys was trapped.

"Sorry Theresa," she tried to sound calm. She hoped she might buy herself a little time to think how to extricate herself from this horrible situation. She had offended Theresa, perhaps, angered her by not complying with her advice and her demands. Now, Cerys could almost touch the hatred spilling from Theresa's very core, and she knew herself to be in danger.

"I was planning to come back," Cerys continued, treading carefully with her words. "I'd every intention…but I've not been feeling too good, you know, how it is with me?"

She pictured the garden behind her, walled in perfectly, the gothic-style iron gate with the key rusted solid in the padlock. With Theresa barring the front door, Cerys's only means of escape was up the stairs. The thought of being trapped up there with the dreadful, heavy atmosphere pressing in around her and Theresa, full of venom and rage, terrified Cerys more than she had ever known was possible.

She wavered for a moment, fear and disbelief at the craziness of the situation rooting her to the kitchen floor.

"Always the same, you...*people*," Theresa sneered, peeling herself away from the door slowly and inching forward. "Come to us for help but the moment the milk curdles or the weather turns bad you blame *us!* Living shoulder to shoulder for generations, *helping you all!* And we gets repaid with what? Drowned in our own well, or hounded out the village and hung off the gibbet in front of a baying crowd of our own neighbours! Always...the fucking...*SAME!!*"

Theresa was inches from Cerys now, her fury seeming to swell her height. She felt Theresa's spittle land upon her brow with the emphasis of her last few words, which she hissed through clenched teeth, her black eyes bulging with ugly rage. Cerys's fractured nerves broke completely as she registered Theresa's sudden proximity and she turned and fled up the wooden staircase, two at a time, falling over her own feet at the top one. She scrambled through her bedroom doorway on her hands and knees and slammed the door shut behind her, her hands shaking terribly as she turned the key to lock it.

Cerys leant against the door, her heart thumping. After a few moments of deafening silence, she sensed rather than heard Theresa's soft footsteps on the stairs, as she ascended cat-like and stopped outside the bedroom door. Cerys's skin prickled with terror, her hand over her mouth, as she battled fiercely to contain her panic.

"What next, Cerys Thomas?" Theresa's mouth was close to the keyhole, her words seeming to float through to the other side like little noxious clouds. *"Are you going to scream? Or call the police?"*

Cerys, crouched below the keyhole, had no words. Her silence now was her only weapon, her only miniscule advantage. Just a little more time, just a few minutes more and someone would come, she would think of something. *"Just hold on,"* the incantation repeated senselessly in her head, over and over. *"Just hold on."*

"What will you say to people, Cerys?" Theresa continued. "What will they think - your uncle, your *mother,* the police, the neighbours, if you call them now? *"Oh, help me, my friend came over to visit me, and now somethin' terrible is about to happen, but I can't say what?!"* Theresa mimicked Cerys's voice, a childish whine. "They'll think you're not right in the head, Cerys. Your mother and your uncle know that already. That's why you came here, isn't it, *Crazy Cerys?* In my day, you'd have been hounded of the village too! Me 'n you'se not so far apart at all!"

Theresa tapped lightly with one long finger upon the door, then scratched at the surface with her nail, up and down, slowly. The sound was like a cockroach chafing inside a wall. Cerys felt sick.

"Let me in, Cerys. *Crazy* Cerys Thomas. You *owe* me. I tried to help you and you *needed* me. Now you owe me."

Scrape, scrape, tap...Cerys felt as if she might truly lose her mind listening to that sinister, insect noise. *Scrape, scrape, tap, TAP* ...she had to get away from it. She crawled over to the tiny built-in wardrobe, empty save for a small heap of her laundry and a row of wire coat hangers which chimed as she squeezed inside.

Cerys pulled the door shut tight and hunched on the floor in semi-darkness, with her knuckles stuffed between her clenched teeth, suppressing the urge to start screaming. She was deeply afraid that if she surrendered to that impulse she might never return to her right mind again. The oppressive energy in the air thickened, as the tapping noises travelled from the outside of the bedroom door to the ceiling over Cerys's little room, then down to floor-level and seemingly around in circles both inside *and* outside of the

86

room. There was a scraping on the window pane, on the roof tiles above Cerys's head, and finally, horrifyingly, on the wardrobe door where Cerys kneeled. *TAP.. TAP... TAP.*

Cerys leant back on her heels, her face upturned, silently begging the shadows for mercy. She felt her heel brace against something hard in her back pocket and remembered her phone was there: *she had her phone!* But who could she call for help, indeed? Theresa was right about that –there was no one. Her uncle was miles away, as was her mother. Definitely not the police. Cerys knew in her heart that Theresa was right about that, at least. There would be sirens and drama with the arrival of a car and all they would find would be one hysterical teen in a big cupboard. She would be sectioned for sure. And the only neighbour in Quaintlip that Cerys had been reasonably acquainted with was dead. Crouched awkwardly on the nest of crumpled clothes on the floor, Cerys shifted position slightly to keep her balance. Her foot stirred the jeans she had worn on Sunday when she had ventured to the parish hall to meet her uncle. The card, with the church lady's name and number on it, was sticking out of the pocket.

Cerys dialled the number without hesitation: she did not have time to consider how appropriate it was to call for help from a virtual stranger. The tapping was growing steadily louder and Cerys was cornered. She was unsure now whether Theresa was inside the bedroom or still out on the landing. She could not ascertain whether the nightmarish presence polluting the atmosphere was connected to Theresa, or whether it was unhappy coincidence that the two were hunting Cerys simultaneously.

Her phone had one bar of battery left. Cerys's hand shook as it rang blandly into her ear. The hair lying at her temples was damp with sweat, her cheeks too: Cerys vaguely realised that tears were streaming from her screwed-shut eyes. The tapping continued; overhead, this

87

time, but Cerys did not dare to look up. The phone beeped its last warning before it emptied completely of power. *"Please pick up, please!"* Cerys whispered into the dark.

"Hello?" A woman's voice, peculiarly bright and normal. Margaret sounded like she had been out in the garden, perhaps, dead-heading flowers or having a late tea with her kids.

"Hello? It's Cerys, Dom's niece. I don't know if you'll remember me. We met last Sunday.."

"Cerys, what happened, what's wrong?" Margaret interrupted, her voice louder now, and full of concern.

"I can't explain, but I need some help here," Cerys rushed her words, trying to beat the failing phone. *"There's a woman here...and I don't know if she's even real. But she's going to hurt me. I know it sounds crazy, and I was really rude to you when we met but..."*

"Are you at your uncle's house Cerys?" Margaret interrupted.

"Yes, yes I am!" Cerys was fully sobbing now, and the hideous noises outside had reached her eye-level where she huddled behind the wardrobe doors.

"I'm on my way," Margaret said, through the phone's final beeps. "Hold on Cerys, just …" The line went dead.

A numbness engulfed Cerys then as the phone screen went blank. Resignation quieted her sobs, and steadied her shaking hands. Her hammering heart and shuddering breath suddenly grew still and calm. She drew herself to her feet, and stood for a moment in the darkness, thinking of nothing at all. Then she opened the wardrobe door.

Theresa stood before her, balanced on her tiptoes in the most peculiar fashion, Cerys observed distantly. She looked like an ungainly ballerina, draped in black, her coal-black eyes burning into Cerys's own with a murderous fire from dark, deep sockets. Somehow, *somehow,* she was inside the bedroom, and the door that Cerys had locked from within had been flung open.

Cerys took a step forward and for one brief second considered the open window to her right. She could throw herself out; she *would* be hurt badly, she knew that. Or worse. But if it meant leaving this awful, evil, consuming atmosphere of terror and darkness and everything to do with Theresa behind then would it not be a freedom worth a few moments of physical agony before blissful unconsciousness took charge? The temptation to simply be outside, and to put distance between herself and Theresa was immensely powerful. Cerys smiled faintly at the thought. And Theresa leapt at her.

Later, with the generosity of time and the space to think about that day, Cerys would recall a very vivid capture in her mind of a snake at that particular moment. It glittered blackly, moving with infinite speed and deadly accuracy as it – she – Theresa - sprang at Cerys , spitting venom and smelling of sulphur. Cerys had no memory of seeing Theresa's face during these few seconds, though she replayed the scene many times in her head. There was only this mental footage of the black snake / phantom that lunged for Cerys from only a few feet away.

With a rigid arm extended, Theresa had Cerys by the throat in an instant, and gripped her windpipe with such ferocity that a corona of white stars bloomed in Cerys's vision. Her eyes bulged. Blood pounded hotly in her face, throbbing as her circulation was compromised. Cerys's arms and feet dangled limply as her body left the floor and she was driven upwards with nauseating supernatural strength. She was sure she would hit the ceiling, and realised that she was fast losing consciousness. Her eyes rolled in their sockets as she fought for a breath that had no chance of squeezing through the demonic grip on Cerys's throat. In the last few seconds, as the crown of her head

brushed ceiling plaster and blackness swarmed in, Cerys heard another woman's powerful voice from below her suddenly. A furious command resonated around the room: *"PUT DOWN THAT DAUGHTER OF GOD THIS MOMENT! IN JESUS'S NAME, I AM TELLING YOU – GET.. AWAY..FROM..HERE !!"*
Cerys crashed to the floor.

*

"Cerys? Cerys love? Wake up, come on, please wake up!"

An unfamiliar woman's voice broke through clouds of sleep; heavenly, effortless sleep. Cerys did not want to be stirred. She groaned and turned her face away.

"Cerys? *Cerys!"* Now Uncle Dom's worried tone, from somewhere close above her head. She half-opened her eyes, alarmed to see his face, upside-down, not six inches from her own. She breathed in deeply and surrendered her blackout completely – her uncle looked terribly pale. Then she remembered why she was crumpled on the floorboards and jolted up into a sitting position, nearly head-butting Dom midway. Her head reeled.

"Oh my God, is she gone, is it gone?" Cerys gasped, clutching her bruised throat with one hand and her uncle's shoulder with the other.

"You're fine, Cerys, you're ok." Dom said from where he knelt beside her. "Thank God. Theresa's gone, you're safe. She made a hasty exit once Margaret arrived." He tried to prise Cerys's fingers from where they dug into his shirt. "Thank God you're alright."

Cerys felt a ridiculous compulsion to laugh suddenly. The awful, oppressive atmosphere had dispelled, the monstrous weight lifted from the room. She realised that warmth was radiating around her and from within her – she knew not where it came from – yet she recalled having been chilled to the bone with terror only a short time ago.

Cerys relinquished her grip on her uncle, aware now that there were two others beside her. She recognised Margaret Russell, who knelt with her hand on Cerys's forearm, her face full of concern. "Cerys, this is my husband, Dex," she said, gesturing to the man next her. "As soon as I got your call I asked him to start praying for you. And he rang some of our people to do the same while we were on our way over here. I knew you were fighting something serious. We needed back-up! I'm so, so glad that you rang me."

"How did you know... how did that even *work?!*" Cerys was bewildered. Her throat burned. "Water?" Margaret's husband offered.

"Please," Cerys replied hoarsely. He nodded, looking over to Margaret and Dom, and left the room. Margaret continued.

" Your uncle spoke to me a little about your sleeping problem. He – we – guessed there was more to it than just a medical issue."

"I'm sorry Ces," Dom interrupted awkwardly. "I didn't know how else to help...You were getting worse since you came to stay, not better. Instinct told me it wasn't a problem that the doctor could sort out. I've known Margaret and Dex for years; they're a pretty militant prayer team."

"It's ok, Unc." Cerys said. "I'm so muddled up right now though!" Laughter spilled out of her then, and she clamped her hands over her mouth as she fought to control her hysteria.

Dex returned with cool water just then, and Cerys sipped, wincing as her damaged throat fought to swallow.

"That place you were working at...albeit only for a short while...well, it has been well-known in Quaintlip for centuries," Margaret said softly. "It sort of sucks people in. Locals have become involved one way or another with the women who've lived there and most often things have ended badly. Suicides, people gone missing, husbands that have met with tragic accidents. The priests over the years listed various funerals and memorials in the church records, for several village folk who reached a violent or undefined end here. But it's not exactly advertised, if you understand? It was a source of shame and superstition for villagers, I imagine – and still is now, for the older generations whose families still belong here. And I couldn't exactly warn you when I met you, Cerys. You'd have thought I was nuts."

"I couldn't even *begin* to explain what was happening in my world to anyone, even before I came to the village." Cerys shook her head in wonder. "It just got worse and worse when I met Theresa. And I thought she understood! I thought she was my friend. But in the end she scared me even more than the other stuff!"

"From what your uncle told me, about the insomnia and the night terrors, you've been suffering from some spiritual attack on a monstrous scale." Margaret said. "When you're without faith, and isolated, and run-down emotionally, it's like having a door open to Satan. Getting involved with Theresa and 'Spell House was like laying down the red carpet to welcome him in."

Cerys shuddered. "Was she real, I mean, did that actually just happen?!" she asked. "Was I actually in danger, or did I just imagine the whole thing?"

"Yes, Cerys, you bloody well were!" Uncle Dom answered, exasperated. "Physically, spiritually. You were in a battle for your soul, don't you realise that?!"

Cerys's head was spinning as she tried to process all that happened. There were a hundred questions that she wanted to ask but she could not co-ordinate her thoughts, except to ask her uncle incredulously, "How did you get here so quickly? You were an hour's drive from here!"

Her uncle shrugged and replied, "Just a hunch, Ces. I didn't feel good about leaving you on your own this morning. Felt a bit .. afflicted. A cloud hanging over me. Call it insight, intuition, whatever, but I ducked out of work early and raced back.

"You had a warning from *Him*," Margaret said gravely. "He equips us with the means to discern all kinds of things, if only we listened. Not many people have come out of their association with that house very well. Not well at all."

"How do I stop...*It*...from coming back though?" Cerys asked, as she struggled to her feet with legs that felt like jelly.

"One prayer at a time, sweet girl." Margaret replied, helping Cerys to stand. "One day, and one prayer at a time."

Epilogue

It was late August, and the hedgerows were full, bursting with blackberries and perfect wild roses with white, heart-shaped petals that promised fat scarlet hips in the Autumn. Tractors rumbled busily in the vast fields surrounding Quaintlip – rain was forecast and the harvest had begun early that year. Glowing orange begonias spilled, limp and exotic and useless, from hanging baskets over the pavement on the high street. In the large front gardens set back from the road further along, gladioli raised their showy flags of candy-pink, hot orange and bruise-purple, against yellowing, clipped lawns.

Cerys was carefully packing up her few things in her room at Uncle Dom's: her laptop, chargers, wash stuff from the elegantly-tiled bathroom, clothes and books accumulated during her stay. Several of these were paperbacks, hastily-ordered and devoured in the days following her ordeal at the hands of Theresa. Margaret had helped her with choosing them: books about intercession, spiritual gifts and supernatural encounters were subjects that Cerys herself would not have even considered relevant to her world until her experiences that summer.

Cerys had found other work throughout the remainder of her stay in Quaintlip. A pleasant elderly couple, with a formal landscaped garden required Cerys to do nothing more strenuous than to plant soldierly rows of bedding plants and to water them frequently, and to cut the already-immaculate lawn front and back. Their regular help was nursing a slipped disc, they said, and Cerys was happy to fill in for a month or so.

She often thought of the wild garden at the other end of the village, of its hidden treasures and dark secrets being slowly strangled once again by weeds and vines. Sad to know that she would never go back there, Cerys thought, or see its true potential revealed. It could have been an astonishing little sanctuary, shielded quietly behind that enormous leylandii hedge.

Cerys also thought of Theresa, often – a sudden ache now and again for her irreverent spirit and a longing to hear her voice, with all its abrupt tones and strange old-country dialect. Despite the terror she had endured, part of Cerys's soul missed the sensation of the rest of the world ceasing to exist when they were in earnest conversation together. These brief moments, however, were hastily suppressed by flashbacks of their last encounter, and in remembering that when Theresa's smile left her face it was as though the sun had gone out and darkness filled the day.

Cerys stuffed the last few things in the top of her crammed rucksack, and smoothed the now-familiar pale blue duvet and pillow one last time. She was just about to leave the room when she suddenly recalled the amulet on its length of leather, unsavoury to the touch, and the little old-fashioned bottle still full of brown liquid that Theresa had pressed into her hand all those weeks ago. They were still slung under the bed, untouched for some time.

"Shit," Cerys cursed, scrabbling under the bed for the items and staring in annoyance at her palms where they now lay, coated in dust.

"What do I do with these?!" It was not an option leave them at her uncle's house for him to find, and question, and be reminded of the unrest that Cerys felt she had brought into his peaceful world here in Quaintlip. She still felt somewhat responsible to an extent, and it weighed on her conscience. She would not be able to bin them here, either, without him spotting the things. But there was no way that Cerys would consider taking them back to London with her. Already, she had travelled far enough in her learning to know that she had to relinquish any ties with the occult, however trivial they might seem.

"Do you need a hand bringing anything down?" Cerys's uncle called up from the foot of the stairs, making her jump as if she had been caught stealing.

"No, I'm good thanks!" Cerys returned cheerily, her eyes sweeping the room one last time. She shoved the amulet and the bottle quickly into her jacket pocket, grabbed her bags and left the room empty and still.

Somewhere between her uncle helping her to her car with the rucksack and a hold-all, a trip back inside the sweet, cool kitchen to double-check that she had unplugged her earphones left on charge there earlier in the day, and a farewell that was rather more emotional than either Cerys or Dom had expected, Cerys discreetly dropped the amulet and the bottle in a single open-handed drop over the low flint wall into old Mrs Devin's front garden.

Since the house had been left empty, the grass there had grown long and wildflowers and weeds now prevailed; daisies and poppies and tall brittle grasses cushioning and concealing the items immediately. Relieved to be free of the dilemma, and the small scene of her goodbye, ever-conscious of neighbours observing in pretend indifference

95

from behind net curtains, Cerys pushed their image to the farthest corner of her mind. She was eager to be away now, to see her mum, and to be on the road with the windows down and the sun on her face.

Milton Keynes UK
Ingram Content Group UK Ltd.
UKHW020326100524
442467UK00011B/209

9 781917 129350